SCANDALOUS

2

Billie Dureyea Shell

SCANDALOUS 2

Copyright © 2022

All rights reserved to Billie Dureyea Shell.

No part of this publication may be reproduced, distributed or transmitted in any form or by any means, including photocopying, or other electronic or mechanical methods, without the prior written permission of the publisher, except in the case of brief quotations embodied in critical reviews and certain noncommercial uses permitted by copyright law. Any references to historical events, real people or real places are used factiously. Names, characters, and places are products of the authors imagination.

Front Cover Image by graphic designer
Billie Dureyea Shell & Kenny Writes

First Printing Edition 2022

ISBN: 978-1-7350234-3-4

A Not to All
My Readers and Fans

What's up y'all I decided to dedicate this book to all the people that ever had a dream and someone tried to steal their Joy. Here's food for thought a mother fucker without a dream will always try to kill yours facts and know this the hate won't always come from outside your circle sometimes, shit A lot of the times it's motherfuckers that smile in your face that's behind you back talking about you 80% of the hate thats thrown at you will be from people you know or that you thought you was cool with don't waste your time trying to be cool with people who cares about what people think haters are breeding just like dogs what I mean by that is this just like a dog or should I say a puppy you can tell what kind of person someone is going to be by their parents so more than likely if someone's a hater they come from a long line of haters there mama and their daddy was haters their grandma and their grandpa was haters so it's in their DNA it was inevitable that they was going to be a hater so let there hate motivate you to be greater haters going to hate it ain't nothing that you can do about it let them do what they do and you continue to do what you do and Shine. I mean who gives a fuck if they don't like you you can't expect everybody to have good taste I'm out don't forget to leave a comment about the book at Barnes and Nobles Amazon or anywhere you buy the book at I love y'all keep your heads up

Author
Billie Dureyea Shell

Acknowledgement

What's up y'all first and foremost I want to thank all my readers for buying the books that I've been putting out and supporting this journey that I'm going on writing. You guys have really made this writing shit something that I love to do the more you read it the more I write it without y'all putting these books out wouldn't even be worth it so I thank y'all and I love you all 2022 is here so let's get it......... To my Lord and Savior Jesus Christ thank you for blessing me with this talent and these skills I love you more than words could ever say you died on the cross for me and I know I wasn't worthy of it, so every day I'm going to try to prove to you that it wasn't in vain. To my mother, Mom I love you more than words could ever say we've been through the storm in the rain and we still here he was the first woman to ever have my back and I will always love you for that you know there's nothing that I won't do for you. And there's not enough money in the world to pay you back for all the shit I sent you through but I hope it was the things I am doing for you now I'm showing you how much you will appreciate it you always be my number one girl I love you Mama. To my little sister Glenda I miss you and I love you, you know I got your back no matter what and no matter what we go through I got to never change. To my beautiful wife and the love of my life Shatoya I never thought and I could find somebody that I would love just as much as I love myself yet a lot more everything that I have is yours and my heart belongs to you you always tell me that I'm the best part of you or little do you know you're the best part of me you get on my nerves and sometime I wonder is that your job. I love you for now forever and for always 1437. Call my kids and it's a lot of y'all so let's start in age order:

Jazmine, Ant'Juan, Devon, David, little Dureyea, Dillon, Alura, Avi, Cameron, Premiere, Shanice, and Anthony I love all of y'all you guys are the reason I smile. To my grandchildren Jordan, little Devon, and little Roman I love each one of y'all to Uncle Woody thank you for all you done in helping me to become a man you will always be my favorite uncle and a person I turned to for advice when this world get too hectic for me. To my cousin Zane R.I.P nigga I miss you more than words could ever express but just know that I'm down here holding it down and taking care of business and I promise you you'll never be forgotten. Call my nieces and nephews I love you all. To my big brother Lawrence thank you for all that you've done for me and showing me how to get it to my even older brother Fred you maybe you crazy but I still love you to my little cousin Cella you know I got you when you need me and I love you we are the fuck we got and we all fuck we need. To My uncle Woody only son R.I.P you messed and we love you and you won't be forgotten. To everybody else I didn't mention it ain't that I forgot you you just you just wasn't worth mentioning to all my dark side niggas you already know what it is keep doing what you're doing. Oh yeah a few shots cuz I don't want these people to think I'm saying fuck them Margo love you little sister Sade Love You Selena love you Shay Shay love you little Brandon and Lil Brian love y'all auntie Chris love you shit I think that's about it now enough of all this mushy stuff let's get to this book I hope you all enjoy reading as much as I enjoyed writing Happy New Year it's 2022 stay safe keep your mess on and let's get this money .....

8

Author Billie Dureyea Shell

Chapter One

Bryan

Holidays were his busiest time of year and he loved every minute of it. Even now, cleaning up his 'workspace,' as he liked to call it, of any blood was more like a scavenger hunt than real work. Dressed in all black from his black skull cap and gloves all the way down to his black boots, the man was on a mission to finish his job with the precision and care that he was known for. In the pitch dark room he shined the black light across the floor looking for any blood or bodily fluids. "Come on...I know something is out there," he grumbled. Finally, in the corner by the door, he found it - one single drop of blood. Spraying a bleach solution he cleaned the lone piece of evidence and turned the lights back on. Stuffing the tools of his trade back into a black satchel bag that hung off his shoulder, he looked over his work. His target sat slumped over her desk, a mid-forties, blonde-haired marketing executive now dead from two gunshot wounds to the head. It was his best work, but she did put up a bit of a fight, hence the need to check the 'workspace' for any blood particles. He made sure to open a window, letting in the cold air and letting out the full stench of evacuated bodily fluids from his latest kill. "Alright. Looks like I'm all clear," he whispered to himself, shutting off the light again and walking briskly out the office door. Down the hallway and to the steps the athletically built man - tall enough to be a star basketball player - seemed to zoom down the ten flights to the first floor. At the bottom, he calmed himself, steadied his breathing, and just as he was about to go outside his phone rang. "Shit..." He jumped slightly, startled by the phone but the name on the screen wouldn't allow him to ignore it. Family first was always the motto so he answered the phone and entered the cold darkness of night. "Hey Clarence...wassup bruh? Where you at? Sounds noisy," Bryan observed as he entered a dark alley towards a busy street where he could get lost in a crowd. Just before he made it to the road, he carefully took out the weapon he'd used tonight and threw it in a sewer grate. He was almost thankful for the cold; gloved hands eliminated fingerprints but they were more suspicious in warm weather. "I'm in an airport. One last trip before the end of the year...you know the hustle doesn't stop." Clarence laughed and so did Bryan "You're preaching to the choir, fam. I'm on the job right now." "Bryan my brother always working and getting his paper. I'm proud of you bruh." They talked to each other like close brothers but they were more like brothers from a different mother. Step siblings from a relationship that hadn't lasted, the men still called each other brother, especially when one of them needed something. "Oh... just working. You know how that goes." Bryan downplayed the situation as he walked through the streets, blending in with the rest of the holiday shoppers in the downtown shopping district. Everyone was so busy getting out of the cold that no one noticed the man dressed in black from head to toe walking through the crowd. He slipped anonymously through the crowd, all of them oblivious to the fact that he had a gun big enough to kill an elephant on his right hip. "Yeah I feel you bruh. You coming over for our New Year's celebration?" Clarence asked. Bryan thought about it as he made it to his all Black CLS Benz, parked a comfortable seven blocks from his target. "Umm...I don't know about that." Bryan surveyed his surroundings making sure he wasn't followed before jumping in the fine German engineering and taking off. "Come on bruh I need a favor from you." "A favor?" "Is this line secure?" Clarence asked before he continued. "Negative...I will need a second line for that. You know that number." Before Bryan could get the sentence out, his second phone began to ring from the cup holder. "Yeah?" he answered "This is secure right?" Clarence asked urgently. "Yep...wassup." "I got a dilemma I need you to handle." "Like what?" Bryan was down for anything from kidnapping to outright murder; he was what some would call a hit man but he preferred being called a problem solver. "I need you to take care of something for me but...it's a little different. You remember my daughter-in law-right?" Bryan thought quickly as he started the car and slowly left the curb. "Which one?" "The younger one..." Bryan had a damn near photographic memory, he could remember anything and could immediately picture the woman in question. "Lanesha, right?" "Yeah that's the one. I need you to... befriend her and get something back for me." "Ahh, like that one chick in college you had me 'befriend' so you could get a better grade." Clarence laughed at that.

Sometimes he forgot about all of their dealings together, some vanilla and some much worse. "Yeah something like that. And she's going to be at the party so…" "Say no more," Bryan answered. "Send me a picture and her info. I'll figure it out." "Aww thanks, bruh. I really appreciate it." "What is this about anyway?" Bryan asked, relaxing a little as he left the shopping district far behind him, along with the skyscraper where his latest victim was slumped over a desk. She wouldn't probably be found until morning and by then he would be so far removed from the area, no one would know where to start with clues. "I got caught up fam…" Clarence hedged. "Be specific." Bryan asked as he shot onto the highway. Merging onto the three lane expressway then shooting past cars like a slingshot in his all black, luxury getaway car. Clarence explained the situation and Bryan listened, filing information into his mind like the human filing cabinet that he was. "So I need you to get close to her. See if you can calm this situation down and maybe if she has companionship then… "Then she won't blow the whistle on you," Bryan said connecting the dots. "Exactly!" Giving his head a small rub he made a quick decision. "Fine…I'll be there." "My brother…thanks fam." "This should square us up on that one situation right?" Bryan hated owing people and he paid back all of his debts but the one he owed his step-brother Clarence was one of his biggest. "Yep, this will make us completely square. You keep her quiet and I'm good." "No dirt naps?" "Nooo...no...not yet at least." Clarence laughed but Bryan found nothing funny. He was completely serious. Killing someone wasn't a laughing matter to Bryan, but he didn't say a word. Instead he just drove, listening to his brother babble for a few minutes. "Alright bruh so I'll see you at my house on New Year's Eve." Clarence finally wound down his steady rant. "Yeah...I'll be there," Bryan said, giving his word and his word was his bond. Rubbing his stubbled chin he thought about what it would take to seduce a woman. He pictured Lanesha, the way she looked the last time he saw her, and he already knew what he had to do. "Alright. See you soon bruh." He had about a week to get ready for his seduction and as he hung up the phone Bryan was already thinking about what he would say. He was the consummate professional and he was unwilling to leave any job to chance, especially when on the job for his family. He would take this just as seriously as a murder-for-hire gig and that meant extensive preparation.

Steering with his left hand he used his right to type Lanesha's name into his phone. Using a special database her address, phone number, and recent social media pictures came up. He now had intel on his latest job, and with that information he was sure to have perfect aim and not miss his target.

Chapter Two

Yvette

As we lay on the living room floor, me smoking a cigarette and Tron staring at the ceiling, I tried to understand why my daughter would give up all of this for old ass Clarence. Clarence whose signature sex move was getting on top every once in a while. But what I saw him doing on that video wasn't the Clarence I knew. He doesn't do shit like that for me. I cried at first and then I got jealous, hate rising up in me til it was in my brain sending me signals to do something. Now, here I was, resting from the aftermath of my decision. "I guess I should get these cameras down...I gotta get out of here," Tron said as he got up. "What's the rush?" I sat up, watching him fumble to get dressed. "I still got some work to do...and Clarence...

Donesha...fuck!" He jumped up as if he had just now realized what we were doing. "I can't believe I did this shit." Shit? My pussy was far from shit, it was gold wrapped in a small package. "But you liked it right?" I asked. He didn't speak at first, instead searching for his jeans, pulling them up over his stained boxers. A DNA test would confirm that my pussy juices and his cum were mixed in to form a beautiful artistic pattern of cum stains on his boxers. "Did you hear me?" "Huh?" "You liked right?" I repeated. He thought for a moment, a small smile starting to crease his lips before he started to shake his head. "Don't shake it off, just admit that you liked this pussy." "Yeah it was good but I'm engaged to your daughter. You're married. We shouldn't have done this." He found his shoes and I watched as he finished getting dressed. Then he found the small stepladder and used it to take down the cameras that were inside the house. It seemed to only take him seconds but when he was done he stood by the door like a little puppy waiting for orders. "Are you leaving?" I asked, disappointed. "Yeah I need to go. But I think we need to figure out right now what this is." I went to him, my naked body fully exposed as I pinned him to the wall. "This is whatever the fuck we want it to be." My lips on his and he didn't move away when I put my hands back into his jeans. "This is my dick now. So when I call...you better come running. Understood?" He stared at me, checking my seriousness but there were no smiles or laughs on my face. This was real life and now that I've let him get a taste he belonged to me, no matter who was in the way. "I hear you but, Yvette, we can't do this. This one time was a mistake and…" He kept going but his lips looked so succulent and pink and all I could see was the look he'd had in his eyes as I pushed his face down between my legs. Now he was standing here talking to me with these lips that had my pussy juices glazed all over them only an hour ago. There was no way he would take that away from me no matter what he said. He belonged to me or else. "You get that...or I'll have to let my daughter see what happened here today," I threatened. "What?" It wasn't hard to bring up the footage of our sexcapade up on the security app. I watched as he held on to my phone speechless, his head shaking more with every position that we moved in until I pulled my phone away from his grasp. "Now this is how we are going to play this. I will call you...and you come running when I say. Got it?" It was a take it or leave it proposition and he had no choice. "Fine...whatever...I just can't believe this shit," he said, rubbing his temples like he was trying to push a migraine away. I wanted to tell him how much I enjoyed my time, and how we could make beautiful love together but my phone rang, stealing the moment. My husband's name appeared across the screen and sucked the joy out of the room. "I have to go…" Tron didn't wait for my permission. He was out the door, running to his car like a ghost was chasing him. "Hello…" I answered the phone with a smile on my face. "Baby I'm sorry for what I did," Clarence blurted out as soon as he heard my voice. I listened to him beg and plead through the phone about how he didn't mean it but was he apologizing for hitting me or fucking my daughter? "I don't know what came over me. Maybe I need to go back to counseling or something...I'm so sorry," he went on. I didn't say a word, just holding the phone listening to his sorry excuses. I wondered how long he and Donehsha had been going on. I thought about all the possible signs and I saw nothing. They hated each other. But now I knew that was an act, nothing was true and everyone in my life was fake. My daughter betrayed me and my husband helped her do it. "Baby do you hear me?" I snapped out of my trance to see that Tron's car was gone and Clarence was still on my line babbling. "Yes I hear you, Clarence. I'm getting tired I need to get some rest." "I'll be home tomorrow, beautiful. Maybe we can talk then." I could have left him now, gotten a divorce and submitted the video of him cheating on me as evidence but I wouldn't get my full pay out. Per the prenuptial agreement I would get almost nothing, even if he cheated. Just a little while longer...play the game for a little while, I told myself. I had a plan but it wasn't for the weak and I could play this game better than anybody. "I love you Yvette and I'm sorry…""I know you do baby. It's okay…" "Really?" I wanted to laugh at his excitement. Hell no it wasn't okay that he hit me but I let him think it was. "Maybe when I get back we can try for a baby one last time." I wanted to laugh at that too. Clarence always wanted to talk about kids. Even though my uterus was closed and would probably be going through menopause soon, I said whatever I could to keep him at ease. No use in spoiling my big reveal before everything was in place. "Yeah maybe we can try one last time this year," I cooed. For a man that was fucking my daughter you would think he would want as little to do with me as possible, but here he was begging me to have a baby. I wonder what he's telling Donesha. "You have no idea how good it feels to hear you say that. I love you baby. I'm all yours for the holidays all the way through the new year." I rolled my eyes at that. I didn't want to be around him non-stop. He had no idea how good it felt to fuck a real man half my age and now I was addicted. But the more my husband thought we were on good terms, the better. Revenge is best served cold anyways.

Chapter Three

Eve

Every hall, floor, nook, and cranny of Homer Seales Regional Hospital was engraved in Eve's brain. She had walked the halls throughout each night for the past few weeks, to move around and clear her mind. Anything to take her mind off her tiny infant who was fighting for her life. Taking the elevator up to the NICU, Eve went about her normal routine. Smiling and saying hi to all the other parents and nurses that were crowded outside the sterilized room. They all seemed to stare at her and Eve pretended not to notice, but everyone knew that today was the last day. Her angel was going home. She hung up her belongings and began the fifteen minute procedure of scrubbing every particle of dirt and bacteria from her hands. An aid appeared, helping her put on scrubs, head cap, and a mask. Soon she looked like a hazmat worker, covered in yellow with white latex gloves on her hands. "You ready?" the woman asked, but Eve would never be ready for what she had to do. Instead of crying and prolonging the inevitable she simply nodded her head, unable to talk for fear the tears would start flowing. The sounds of machines buzzing and the faint swoosh of ventilators was the soundtrack of the NICU. Eve stepped slowly over to the miniature heated dome that was what her daughter had known as home since the premature delivery. Usually the tiny dome would be dark, filled with tubes, tape, and gauze. But today the lights were on and her little baby was no longer attached to machines but instead dressed and peaceful in a small pink dress. No more cords, tubes, or ventilators were in the way, just a tiny baby with her eyes closed, like a small princess taken away before she could begin. "She looks like she's just sleeping," Eve said from behind her hospital issued mask. Six weeks and her baby girl fought a good fight but now she was resting for eternity with the angels, up in the stars. Today she had finally been called home. "You know her dad didn't come see her... not once." Eve's her voice cracked as she spoke to baby Neveah's nurse. "I named her Neveah because it was Heaven spelled backwards. Now she's in Heaven and he never got to meet her. He didn't come, not even when I told him that this would be happening." Eve wanted to cry, she felt the aching in her eye sockets and intense weight on her chest but no more words would come out. "Yeah she looks peaceful. We got her dressed up for you just like you asked. The priest should be on his way soon," the nurse told her, but there was no need. She just wanted to be alone with her daughter. "Do you want to hold her one last time?" the nurse asked. She wasn't sure if it was healthy to hold her baby's dead body but this would be the only time she would hold the small child without the interference of tubes and machines. "Sure…" Eve sat down in the rocking chair as the nurse placed the peacefully deceased angel in her arms. She had grown a bit since she was born but not enough. There had been too many complications following a risky surgery due to an infection. A week ago the doctors told her there was nothing else they could do. Baby Neveah had fought all she could, but the time was drawing near. "She looks really pretty in this outfit," Eve said as she traced her fingers over the preemie clothes. Neveah was so small that the small outfit sagged on her but it was better than the white hospital issued onesies that she had worn constantly. "I'll leave you alone with her." The nurse left the pair alone as Eve rocked the small baby back and forth. She searched the infant's face for features that were like her own but she couldn't find one. It was as if she hadn't even given birth to the child. From the top of her little head to the bottom of her feet she saw nothing but Tron. "It's okay baby. He'll figure out one day that he missed out on something special with you." She kissed the small cheek. Where she used to feel warmth was now turning colder and heavier by the second. Her baby was gone, she knew that now. The time passed and, although it had felt like only minutes to Eve as she rocked the baby back and forth, several hours went by before the nurses came to intervene. "It's time now, Eve. We need to take her now," they said. Taking her meant putting her in the morgue. They tried not to say those words but Eve knew what they meant. "But I don't want her to go….I can't believe she's gone." "Do you know what arrangements you will make yet?" asked a nurse, kindly. With so little money, her only option was cremation. That was another thing that pained her soul, to have her little princess burned and ground to dust because her father didn't care enough to send money for a proper burial. "I'll have her cremated and from there…I'm not sure," she admitted as she placed her baby girl down in the plastic crib. She said her goodbyes, giving her a kiss on the cheek. The nurse gave her a hug, a long embrace after spending six weeks together talking, crying, and laughing. Caring for Neveah had created a small bond between the two women. They let go of each other and without a word Eve left, trying to leave the hospital without breaking down on the way to her car. She took off her scrubs in a daze, throwing it all away in trash cans as she left. There was no one waiting to take her home like in the movies. There was no long line of people coming with her to talk out her situation. Instead she walked to her car alone, thinking of all the things she had done wrong in her pregnancy. Partying into her eighth week when she realized she hadn't seen her period. A haphazard home pregnancy test that she stole from the dollar store gave her two blue lines instead of one. A clue that she was pregnant, but how could she have a baby? Eve was barely twenty-one, with no money, living in a studio apartment, struggling to pay rent. But sure enough, a trip to the clinic confirmed that she was one hundred percent with child. Telling Tron was okay at first. He seemed excited, taking her to dinner and going away for a nice weekend. But the next week she couldn't reach him and when she did, he said one sentence that crushed her soul. "I think you should get an abortion." The A word hadn't even crossed Eve's mind until he said it. When she refused he went into a rage, telling her that he would never be there and she would raise the baby on her own. "How am I supposed to tell my gal about this?" she heard him mutter when he thought she wasn't listening. She was so busy crying that she never told him that she heard those words, she never had a chance to make him apologize. He hung up that day and refused to take her calls. Tracking him down at work was the only way to put a stop to her endless worry. But when she finally saw him the unthinkable happened. She went into early labor brought on by the undue stress. Now she was getting into her cold car, her hands still smelling of the hospital antiseptic and almost numb as she tried to start her car. Everything was numb from her brain down to her feet so she barely could feel the gas pedal as she drove out of the parking lot. As she drove, she kept taking a long sniff of her hands, bathing her senses in the smell that reminded her of her firstborn. That smell would forever sit in her memory, linking her to a daughter that would never come home. That thought was stuck in her brain and now, in the comfort of her car, the thoughts finally became too much. She cried, the tears coming down as she held her stomach, where her baby should still have been. She wasn't due for another two months - a lot of time for a baby to grow and mature to be ready for the world. "I'm sorry I robbed you of that...I'm sorry that I was thinking about him and not about you," she sobbed, barely able to get the words out through her tears. From the hospital parking lot all the way to her house she cried and cried, endless tears that seemed to get worse and worse. Inside she checked into what was more like a jail than a studio apartment. All around were the reminders that she was supposed to be a mother. A crib sat in the corner and various baby clothes were there as well. Lying in bed she cried and cried with no one to console her and tell her it would be alright. She cried until she got sick. She cried herself to sleep and when she woke up she cried some more. Alone in her apartment with the shades drawn, she tried to find herself or at least figure out where she made the wrong turn. Every time she tried to track the problem she always ended up back in the same place. "Tron...it's all your fucking fault." She stared at the picture of them both that sat on her nightstand. The picture from one of their dates, basking in each other's company and seeming so deep in love. Little did she know it was all a show, a lie, and she was the side chick being used by a classic manipulator. "You lied to me...you told me that you loved me and you cared about me then...then you deserted me," she told the picture but it was stuck in time. Stuck back in the time when she knew nothing about the real Trontavious. "But you lied to not just me...you lied to us." She threw the picture and it landed perfectly in the middle of the dozen or so mementos scattered across her bed. Photos, documents, reports, and a DNA test request lay across her bed painting a picture of the man she had called her lover - Mr. Trontavious Carter. "I hate you...I fucking hate you!!" she screamed at his photographed face, but that didn't do her anger justice. She had vowed not to do this but after being ignored she had no choice. She leaped up to her feet and went in search of her phone. With the sun just now setting, Eve grabbed her phone and dialed the number she had memorized. "Hello, Auto Sales, this is Jessica..." "Yes I need to speak with Trontavious Carter, please." The phone went silent, no clicks, rings, or a request to hold on. Instead there was nothing but awkward silence on the line. "Hello?" Eve looked at the receiver making sure the call hadn't dropped. "Hello…" "Yes…yes ma'am," the receptionist's responded, her move to unmute the line was way more obvious than she tried to make it and pushing Eve further to the end of irritation. "May I ask who's calling?" "Why?" Eve snapped back at her, more annoyed by the second. "Can't you just put me through?" Why does it matter who it is? "Umm…I'm sorry ma'am," the receptionist said robotically, like she was reading from a script. "Trontavious no longer works here." The wheels in Eve's head started turning. He told her to say this. He is avoiding me, she told herself as her anger began to rise. "What do you mean? He was working there a month ago…now all of a sudden poof…he's gone?" She looked at the phone as if she were being tricked in some way. "Put Tron on the phone, bitch," he growled into the receiver, wishing she could jump through the phone and strangle the receptionist with her bare hands. "Excuse me ma'am…Don't curse at me." Thoughts of her lost child tumbled around in her head and in an instant Eve's temper exploded through her mouth and into the phone. "PUT TRON ON THE PHONE, BITCH!" she screamed but before she was done pronouncing the last syllable the phone went dead. "FUCK!" Throwing the phone on the bed she balled her fist up and sent it through the wall. Plaster and drywall dust covered her arm as she screamed, wishing that the hole was in Tron's head instead of in her bedroom wall. "He's there. He just doesn't want to talk to you," she reasoned with herself, but that line of reasoning was unacceptable. "No...no... no… that's still not a reason," she told herself back. She needed him to understand that this wasn't right. "Regardless of that, he still missed her birth. He missed everything. Now she's gone and he never even knew her name!" She began to cry, seeing flashes of the life she had planned go up in smoke then reappear as her dead daughter dressed in pink. The shaking and crying made her knees buckle as she sobbed, crying out for help. Eventually the tears dried and the choking stopped and Eve was left holding her legs and rocking back and forth with a focused gaze on the nightstand picture. After a while the picture became real to her. He wasn't in an inanimate frame but was an actual person held in time inside her bedroom. With the same smile and expression, he stood in front of her with a cheesy grin. "After all you've put me through. You're just going to smile?" she asked the hologram Tron that was now growing bigger in her space. "You know what Tron… I'm going to make you wish that you never met me. That you had never been born. And I'm going to make you regret missing my child's life. With everything in me I will make you suffer you sonofabitch!" Eve yelled, jumping to her feet. In her reality she was grabbing Tron by the throat, squeezing it until the smile faded away but what she was really holding was the broken picture frame with broken glass cutting through her hand. A crunched picture of Tron was in the middle of the mess, covered in Eve's own blood as the glass ripped through her soft skin. She wanted to scream from the pain, from the sight of her own flesh being torn apart by Tron but the screams wouldn't leave her mouth. In fact, her lips wouldn't even part. Instead she walked calmly to the bathroom. Grabbing peroxide, bandages, and tweezers she removed the bits of glass with the precision of a surgeon, one by one without making a sound. The picture of Tron was now scratched and stained with blood and Eve had no intention of changing that. She didn't even bother to wash off the blood. "That's how your ass deserves to be. Covered in blood you bitch…" She coughed and spit a perfect glob of her saliva onto the picture. Looking in the mirror, the bags under her eyes, messy bun, and scraggly eyebrows meant nothing. She had a calling now, something she had to do. It was clear in her spirit that Tron needed to be taught a lesson. He had to pay, and the best way to do that was to pour every bit of energy she had into his demise.

Chapter Four

Donesha

After several needle sticks and spreading my legs for a tissue sample I was now waiting. They said they would have some results today so I tried to stay calm and not read the scary disease information covering the exam room walls. All this information on everything from Syphilis to HPV was littered everywhere giving me a million ideas of what could be going on. Please God don't let me have a disease. Anything but that, I prayed as I waited. I tried shifting my mind to other things, like my wedding. I wanted royal purple and gold as our colors but Tron wanted red and white. I wanted to get married within the next year but he wanted to wait a few years. Things weren't matching up and I guess I had no way to tell him he was wrong. Here I was in a clinic getting a checkup because of another man. A man that was my mother's husband. The shit sounded sick when you said it all together. Every thought I had was from one extreme of fucked up to the next. "Alright…" The doctor swooped in with a few papers in her hand. She smoother her jet black hair in its ponytail and pushed her gold wire-rimmed glasses back onto the bridge of her nose. "We have to wait about a week to get the pap results back and around the same time for the blood work," she said with her Russian accent so thick I could barely understand her. "That's fine...but what about..?" I pointed to the papers. "Is there anything in there about the Trick that I asked you about?""Yes. You are positive for trichomonas." "WHAT?!" I screamed, as if she had given me the disease. "Not to worry, we just have to give you a prescription and you will be good as new. In your condition just taking the pill form will be fine to clear things up." My condition? The doctor acted like this was nothing. I prided myself on being disease free and now I had something. Fucking Clarence. I'm going to fuck him up. I felt like running out of the office and beating his ass right now. How am I going to tell Tron he needs to get treated? "I feel sick...I think I'm going to be sick." A nurse knocked on the door seconds later. A tray of medicine and a needle confirmed that they were very serious about what she had told me. "Wait a second. We have to make sure that won't interfere with the other situation," the doctor cautioned. My ears perked up when I heard that. "Is that all? Is it something else?" Did I have herpes or something? "Oh you're right…just pills for her." The nurse said putting the needle back on the tray with a smile. What the hell is she smiling about? "What is going on?" Somebody better tell me something or I was going to flip out really quick. "We tested your urine and it came back positive for HcG. The pregnancy hormone." Now she was just messing with me. I had to laugh at that. "No ma'am. You see, I knew you had the wrong results." I shooed her away, laughing at the audacity of this lady. "You have to do better than this doc. You can't go around giving out false results." This is what I got for coming to the free clinic, but I had waited long enough, three whole weeks since I heard my Mama say that Clarence had a disease. I had fucked him since then without a condom, further proving how stupid I was. Now I was here to take care of my health and they feed me this bullshit. "Why do you say that? These came from your tests." This so-called doctor didn't know me or my history and if she did she wouldn't have come to me with these lies about a pregnancy test. I probably would have believed her. "Ma'am...I was molested when I was a child. I was told that I would never have kids so please. Go get my real results." These damn clinic doctors never seemed to care. They were so careless, even giving me the wrong damn test results. She paused and cleaned her glasses with her white physician's coat but that still wasn't enough to get her to see my side. "When was your last period?" I shrugged, she was still reaching for something to prove this lie. "I don't know whatever I wrote on the paper. I'm damn near in med school so I don't have time to keep up with my period anymore," I laughed, just being happy to have on matching clothes and shoes. "Okay, I'll be right back." She and the nurse left just as quickly as they came and I started to walk out right behind her. But I waited. I wanted to see the look on her face when she figured it out and that she was going to have to apologize. A few moments later, the door cracked a bit then shoved open by doctor, now pushing a cart. I saw a monitor and something in my brain finally registered that this was an ultrasound machine. "We double checked and these are your results Ms. Hill. And we will do an ultrasound to confirm that." I didn't have time to think. They were already plugging up the machine and slathering my stomach with a cool gel. "I told you...I'm not pregnant this is just..." But then I saw it. I watched the screen and a little cell stuck out like a sore thumb. "Yep, there you have it. You are pregnant." She rolled the ultrasound wand around a bit to get a better angle. This morning when I left the house I wasn't expecting any of this and now I was in tears watching a small monitor with my baby on it. "This isn't real...there is no way," I whispered. "Do you want me to print one for you?" she asked. "No...I want you to tell me how is this possible." "Are you okay Ms. Hill. Do you need water?" the nurse asked but I didn't need shit but the truth. "I was molested when I was younger. The doctors...they have always said that...I could never..." I thought back to that time and instantly the tears came sprouting out of my eyes. This was a part of my life that I had tried to bury but still I remembered vividly the number of tears I cried after hearing I would never have kids. As a child you can't fully wrap your mind around the concept but as I got older my hate and anger towards that day and time brought more and more understanding. I was barren, excruciating periods were all I had left and because of that I wished every day that my grandmother could come alive and die again. It was all her fault that this happened and now her spirit was toying with me. "Do you know why the doctors said that specifically?" the doctor interrupted my thoughts. "Something about scaring and trauma. I'm not exactly sure but I know they said it wasn't possible." She hit a button on the machine and a small printer began to buzz. "Are you sure you're okay Ms. Hill? You are shaking." Looking down at my hands, they were trembling but this was equivalent to being told you are going to die and someone comes back and says that you were fine the whole time. "Well, whatever was wrong has now been corrected." She passed the small ultrasound picture to me. "You are going to be a mother." Holding the picture I felt joy for a fleeting instant before a problem came into my thoughts. "Do you know how far along I am?" My mind raced like a rapid fire rolodex trying to figure out what dates I fucked who on. Some days I overlapped. I would see Tron in the morning and Clarence that night. It was a crazy time of ho activities that I wouldn't have admitted to my closest friend. I wasn't proud of it but now there was a child, a child that could belong to my fiancé or to my mother's husband. The thought alone made my head hurt. "Looks to be about eight weeks from calculations." Eight weeks, I needed a calendar. I needed to know what happened eight weeks ago and who I was with. "Congratulations." Everything else she said was just like a mumble. I tried to pay attention but none of it mattered anymore. I prided myself on being clean, never having a disease and now I was just like all those women I talked about. How could I have been caught slipping? It had to be Clarence, there was no way that Tron was messing around. That made things even worse. Out of the clinic I walked like a mechanical robot to my car and sat there in a daze. There was a new life inside me and as sat there, I didn't know where to go first. Who knew if Tron was the daddy or if it was Clarence? I was diseased, pregnant, and confused about who got me this way. And that worst part was that I didn't know how to get out. I was all set to drive home and drown myself in the bathtub when my phone rang. "Hello?" I answered. "Yes...is this...Donesha?" I didn't recognize the voice and no number showed on the screen. "This is she." As soon as I said that, the woman started laughing. "What can I do for you?" This felt weird and with all the things that were now swirling in my head I didn't have the time or the patience for anybody's bullshit. "You can't...not yet. But you will soon." Then the phone went dead.

Chapter Five

Iron

I've cheated on Donesha more times than I could count and it always went the same way. I got my dick wet then I came home, took a shower, and I was back to myself. But not after Yvette. I couldn't stop thinking about her, she had turned me into some tender, dick ass little boy after just one time. I don't know what it was, maybe how she challenged me, slapping me across my face. IT made me mad enough to hit her but instead I gave her a dick lashing. I've never been a tender dick about a bitch but somehow she stayed on my mind. I don't know if it was the sex or maybe it was the money she told me about. Either way, I tried my best over the last few weeks to stay away. After that first time, I told myself I would never do that again. I got good at avoiding her, spent Christmas with my side of the family and planned on telling Donesha that I wanted to stay at home by ourselves this New Year's Eve. But somebody else had other plans. It was like she read my mind when she sent me a text to meet up and talk. The message was simple, meet her on the edge of town to talk. A talk turned into an agreement and on that cold chilly morning the agreement lead me to this hotel. It had outdoor hallways and wall unit air conditioner but it had a bed and a bed was all we needed. Now I was breaking her back on New Year's Eve. "Fuck me...Fuck me Tron..." Her voice bounced off the cheap motel walls. Our clothes were scattered around the room as I bent her ass over grudge fuck style. I was giving her my signature move where I grab a fist full of a bitch's hair and hold on tight as I grind into her ass from behind. The pope...Jesus...even my own damn mother could have told me that I was going to be fucking my girl's mom and I would have laughed at they ass but the proof was in the pudding, or the pussy rather. Because I was dick deep in Yvette as she called my name. "Tron...oh Tron..yes...Like that baby...right there." Chicks went wild when I put in my signature move of ass grinding and pelvis pumping but none of them went wilder than Yvette. She screamed and hollered, making me feel like

I had the biggest dick in the world. Usually I had to do all the work but with Yvette, we moved as one. "Shit girl..." She pushed her ass back into me. Her pussy so wet and soft that my dick was swimming in a marshmallow. I held on as she took control popping her pussy back on me as she led my free hand around the front of her to play with her clit. "Yes...yes...just like that." She encouraged me as we kept moving together in our own little grind bounce dance. The room spun and my heart pounded like a snare drum. I felt the cum rise up and within seconds I was exploding inside of her. "Yes daddy...come inside me." I felt like a king as she pushed her pussy back on me while I filled her with my seeds. "Oh shit..." I pulled out as I came out of the trance. "I came in you. I'm tripping...fuck fuck fuck..." We had done that at least twice, popping through all of our condoms when we decided that skin to skin was the best way, like the first time we met. Now all these weeks later I couldn't keep my hands off her. "Don't worry. I'm taking birth control still. It's okay." She smiled, so sure, as she panted out of breath. "I like it when you cum in me anyway. When Clarence tries to go down on me I imagine he's sucking your nut out of my pussy." "Damn girl...I don't want to imagine that." It was like a bull had head butted me in the stomach. "I'm just saying I don't respect his ass. You're a real man...I just wish..." She looked away, not wanting to say it. Neither of us talked much about the whole arrangement. We just moved like two secret lovers, booking motels on the edge of town or sneaking in text messages on apps that held no names. It happened so quickly it was hard for me to even digest it. One minute we were just son-and mother-in-law, now we were...fucking. "How long...?" I tried to find the words but we had to talk about this. "How long do you think we are going to do this?." She shrugged at that. Patting a towel between her legs she just kept fanning herself like she didn't have a care in the world. "Do you even care if we get caught?" I asked. "You see...I'll answer your question like this. People all around the world are doing fucked up shit. This one thing that I'm doing here isn't going to change the course of history." She was extremely cynical when she wanted to be but sweet at other times. "But Clarence and Donesha..." "Fuck them...We keep doing what we're doing but don't mention them to me okay," She snapped and I thought she was going to bite my damn head off. It was an honest question for someone having an affair, but to Yvette whatever I said was fighting words. "Look

I'm just under a lot of stress with lawyers and…" She started talking about court dates but I had no clue what she was talking about. "Are you in some kind of trouble or something?" I began to sit up looking around as if the FBI had the room tapped. I always wondered how her husband made his money. Sometimes I joked with Donnie that his ass was going to get locked up one day. She hated when I said that shit. "No…" Yvette laughed. "I guess it's not funny though. But my Moms will. There was…well…" She looked away. "What…did she leave you a house in Europe or some shit?" I had to make her laugh. The situation with granny dying was crazy. One day she was walking around cursing people and the next she was in a coma. "No, she left me and the girls about six hundred thousand dollars." I almost fell off the bed when she said it. "What? Are you fucking serious." "Chill…" She shook her head as she put her bra on. "What do you mean chill? That's a lot of fucking money." "I know, that's why I'm not in a rush to give it to the girls. I know they might blow right through it." I thought about Donesha and her crazy ass spending habits. She could make a hundred dollars disappear in ten seconds. "So what are you going to do?" "Well, I have a prenup with Clarence. I just have to stick with his ass for five years and I get everything. So I'm going to save my inheritance money and try to push this out as long as possible so it's not included in the divorce." "What?" "Yeah I don't want it included." "But what about Nene And Lonnie?" "What about them? They're fine." "But they need money. Hell, Nene is going to be in med school. I'm supposed to make a five thousand dollar payment in a few months." Since I lost my job I had no clue where that payment was coming from. "She does...I don't give a damn about what she needs to pay for." She stormed off going into the bathroom slamming the door. "Yvette...don't be like that." The faucet turned on and she locked me out, leaving me with my dick swinging in the hotel. Six hundred thousand dollars divided by three people was a lot of dough. It was enough to put a down payment on my own dealership and get a lot of shit taken care of. She came out of the bathroom with her lip poking out. "What's wrong?" "You're judging me. I didn't know I was going to fall in love with you and…" "What's that on you?" I turned her around looking at her back and saw a bruise I didn't notice before. "Oh... that's nothing." She quickly tried to cover it up but it was too late. "Nothing? It's red and black. Did you hit something?" She froze like a deer in headlights as I examined her. "Were you in a car accident?" She moved away from me as I touched it, wincing in pain. "Did Clarence…" "Just leave it alone." "Are you fucking serious?" I shouldn't have cared but for some reason thinking of him putting his hands on her made my face hot. "Just leave it be. I'm going to leave him soon enough." "But what if he beats the hell out of you in the meantime?" I had questions and it seemed she just wanted to leave it alone. "Trust me he isn't going to do that. I just want to enjoy our time, I already have a plan to get them back." "Them?" "Him and the bitch he's fucking with. Don't worry about it. The shit is a long drawn out story that I don't want to talk about right now. She had more secrets than a damn diary. Watch out playa. These chicks gone get you fucked up. I heard Ro in my head and now sitting in the position I was in, I could believe him. I hadn't talked to him since I got fired. He would be really surprised to hear about the shit that I was into now. You know what…I'm going to take a shower real quick." I watched her now and I could see where Donesha got her ass from. What the fuck are you doing? I felt like I was floating in a cloud. Losing my job and her getting me drunk life just seemed to spiral and before I knew it we were fucking. What was I supposed to do? I played a game over the last few weeks. What would happen if Donesha found out? I went from a few different extremes. In one, Donesha would stab me in my sleep; the other was of her crying, crushing her life and heart into a million pieces. You could have left...my mother...MY FUCKING MOTHER. I would try to console her but what could I say. "Baby I was over your mom's house and she was massaging me and somehow my dick came out." She would kill me, no way she wouldn't. As if she felt me talking about her, my phone rang filling up the hotel room. "Didn't I tell you no cell phones?" She was in the shower but somehow she heard my phone as soon as it started ringing. "Tron turn it off." "Chill,"s you're daughter." The bathroom door slammed like she was some fucking teenager. It was like the bitch was trying to run me. "Hello..." I heard nothing but crying, the muffled tears of Donesha. She knew, she had to know. I sat up in the bed waiting to hear her screams. "Donesha... what is it? Talk to me baby." "I need to see you...I need to see you right now." "What's wrong?" "Right now Tron. Get home please, I can't talk to you about this over the phone." "Okay...I'm on my way." Hanging up, I got dressed like I was going to my funeral. Coming out of the bathroom, Yvette instantly started going off. "Where the hell are you going? I told you no cell phones. I can't believe this shit…" She took the wooden hangers from the hotel closet and started tossing them at me like basketballs. "Yo what the fuck is wrong with you!" "I can't believe you…" She cried like I was the one that beat her. She acted like I raped her. I watched and took cover. "Yo chill the fuck out Yvette…what is wrong with you?" "Just leave…this was a fucking mistake. Just leave." She ran back into the bathroom slamming the door like I was chasing her. "Just leave. I can't believe I did this shit." I wanted to go after her, see what the hell her problem was but between my phone ringing and the sound of glass breaking in the bathroom I put my clothes on and raced out of there. You've fucked up this time Tron." Ro was in my head again. It was like everybody was in my damn head except me. My phone rang again, trying to make it down to the lobby had my snapping as I answered. "WHAT?!" Instead of tears, crying, or yelling I heard laughter. "Who the fuck is this?" "I know you better take some of that bass out ya voice nigga." The crackling of his voice let me know who it was instantly. "Yo Melo…Wassup man. My bad I thought…" "Have you thought about my money?" "Umm. I haven't forgot dawg I…" I tried to explain as I waited for the elevator but he wouldn't let me. At every explanation he stopped me. Changed my words around on me. "You shouldn't forget owing a nigga twenty fucking thousand dollars." "Yeah dawg. I know but…" "But what nigga? I should have had a payment a week ago." I stopped talking and started listening. "What, you ain't got shit to say?" "Naw man… I don't for real." "Well word on the street says you got fired from your job. You fucking up double time. I had some cars I had planned for over there." That was the other half of my dilemma. Me losing my job fucked a few ventures I had going on. Not just my money but side hustles that ran through the dealership. "FUCK…" everything was falling down on me at one time. I needed a lot of money and real fucking fast. I had only one way to get it and back in that hotel room was the pussy that held all the money. Fuck her out of it. Shit goes south at least you got the money. With slow steps I walked back, turning my cell phone off. Back in the room she was out of the bathroom now sitting on the bed naked, her makeup running. "Why are you back?" She looked delicate like a flower and I was a honey bee coming to sting her ass. "I just wanted to see if you were okay…I wanted to make sure that there was nothing bad between us…" I eased back into the room choosing my words carefully like a pastor in a full church. "I'm just sorry...I'm sorry if you're hurt and that this happened." "I give...I give everything to everyone else and I get stepped on. By my husband...by my fucking kids. My mother is gone and...I'm just alone. No one gives a damn." I went to her, wrapping my arms around her as she cried digging her nails into my back as she cried. "I'm sorry...I'm so sorry." I felt the heat from her body. The volcano of her heart exploding and here I was trying not to get burned. A phone rang but it wasn't mine. Instead hers vibrated on the bed and she went to it instantly, shielding herself with a sheet. "Yes...yes...Yes I can do that. Okay... Yes. I'm the executor of the estate. Right...okay." In seconds she was off and a smile stretched across her face. "You okay...?" "I'm more than okay." She said smiling. "The insurance money...We got more than I thought." "Really...How much?" "Three...three hundred thousand." I damn near fell to my knees. "Shit..." "They want to settle everything now..." "So what are you going to do?" "I don't know. I still don't want to tell the girls yet. I want to get things set up for them first." I started counting. As she said it. Something just occurred to me. I had something going with all three of them. What if... "Nine hundred thousand dollars...Split three ways." She started crying again but this looked like tears of joy. "If Mama didn't do shit, she did one thing right." I had the thought but how the fuck could I pull it off. If I could get fifty thousand from all three of them and keep the shit quiet it would change everything. I could pay off Rollie and…" "TRON!" "Huh…yeah…" "Did you hear me…?" "Naw I'm sorry I was…" "What should I do? Should I tell the girls or keep this to myself?" I didn't have a plan yet. I needed a plan and I needed to talk to Lanesha first. "Just hold on to this. Hold off for a minute. What about your husband?" "Fuck him…I'm yours now." She said kissing me deeply in my mouth, like we were getting married. "Ain't that right?" How could I tell her no? If I did, my whole world would blow up more than it was now. I had to have something to hang on to. "Yeah you're right baby. It's you and me." I lied like I did to all females, but she wanted more. "So you're going to leave her. When I leave Clarence of course." She put me on the spot like I was sitting on trial. Her eyes on me, nowhere to run or hide. I had to secure one of them. Out of the three, Yvette was the most important. She controlled all of the bags while Lanesha and Donesha took what was given to them. I was flying above myself again looking down on the disaster. Not only did I kiss her but I pulled away the sheet. Pushing her back on the bed I traced my hands down over her body as I went to my knees. Eye level with her snatch I pulled her to the edge of the bed. With a smile I pushed my head face first into her juicy center as she clawed at the bed. It wasn't right, I was dead ass wrong, but I needed this and there was already no turning back. I was all into this shit. Now I just had to make this bitch cum to secure my future then make it home to Donnie.

Chapter Six

Lanesha

I raced to the house getting there just as Tron was pulling in behind me. I hadn't seen him since the day I bailed him out of jail. He still hasn't gave me my money back, but I wasn't here to talk about that today, I needed to find out what was going on with my sister, but seeing him frantic made the alarms pop off in my head. She knows. "Hey?" he said as I got out of the car. He had a shit look on his face like he was guilty of something. "What's going on?" "Happy new year to you too…" I rolled my eyes at that. He still looked good in his suit and I could smell his intoxicating cologne from where I stood a few feet away. But that was as close as I wanted to get to the man. I told myself if he didn't come around before the clock struck midnight on the new year then we would be done. And here we were a week into the new year and I hadn't heard a word from him. "What's going on? Why am I here?" I asked him, avoiding the lame flirting that he liked to do. "I don't know...she called and told me to come home, that it was something she needed to talk to me about." "She said the same thing to me. You don't think that she knows about...you know?" He looked around for a second up to the house and shrugged his shoulders. "Only one way to find out." We both walked to the door. Me behind him because if we walked into an ambush I was going to let his ass get hit first. But instead going into the house there was light jazz playing, incense lit, and my sister on the couch with a smile from ear to ear. "Baby what's going on?" He went to her, hugging her like I wasn't even in the room. Relax he isn't you're man, I had to tell myself so I could stay calm but a big part of me wanted to slap him in the face for disrespecting me over and over again. I'm cool enough to fuck, bail him out of jail, and be his on call concubine but I'm not good enough to be his companion. Seeing them hugged up made me want to throw up but I swallowed my pride and gave my sister a hug. "What's up Sis are you okay?" Our relationship was rocky since the Thanksgiving night reveal of her relationship with Clarence, if that's what you would call it. She hadn't clarified exactly what they were to me. And since I figured out that Tron wasn't worth fighting for I stopped caring. Now I was in her living room sitting down on her loveseat pretending that I don't want to jump in her man's arms and kiss him all over. "I just wanted my favorite people around me." She smiled a little devilish grin. "That's it baby?...you had me rush home." he tickled her and she squealed like a toddler as they played. I cleared my throat letting the love birds know I was still in the room and had no intention of watching them make out. "Okay, well sis I love you. I'm gonna head out." I turned to leave seeing that whatever she wanted must have been some type of false alarm. "Hold on..." She laughed. "Why are you leaving so soon? I cooked for you." "Oh yeah, baby, you cooked?" Tron asked taking off his suit jacket, a nice fresh hickey on his neck. I glared at it. "What? So now you want us to eat." This was making no sense, she was making no sense and seeing Tron all over her and affectionate was making my ass itch. "Yep, go get the food out the oven. Baby go help her." She pushed Tron towards the kitchen with me. I felt this was a setup but we smiled and walked slowly into the kitchen anyway. "It's in the oven." Tron at my side walking slow right along with me. "Is it a bomb?" he whispered laughing. Everything was a joke to him, but I ignored his dumb ass and pulled open the oven. "Ohh shit." A set of rolls with an ultrasound sat on the top rack. "BABY!!!!" he screamed, running back in the living room. "We're having a baby!" I could hear them laughing, Tron screaming, but in my heart I was crying. Fix your face, be happy. Taking the ultrasound back in the living room. the first thing I saw was Tron's smile. The expression across his face was joy like I've never seen, even when we were together in our most intimate moments. "Congratulations!" I pretended to be excited. Screaming and jumping up and down even squeezing out a few fake tears. "How do you feel?" "I feel good. A little tired. I don't think I'm going to Mom's party tonight. Don't feel like talking to her. Don't know if she's going to be happy or tell me that I'm screwing up by not being done with school." "Well...I gotta go because she wants me to pick up some things," I lied. I had to go before I cried in her face and slapped the dreads off Tron's head. "But I love you. Can't wait to see my little niece or nephew." I rubbed her stomach as if something could be felt already. "Alright sis...Love you," she said squeezing me tight. I wanted to ask her if was she sure the baby was Tron's, but who knew at this point. I was done trying to connect the dots and as Tron sat beside her on the couch, he couldn't even look me in the eye. "Is it okay if I tell Mom or do you want to tell her?" She thought about it for a moment. "You can tell her." "Alright...love you. Boy, this is a happy new year's gift for real." I backed towards the door waving and smiling but once I made it out into the cold, I ran to my car. I jumped inside and burned rubber, right as the tears began to fall. "You're so stupid...stupid...stupid...stupid," I told myself, banging on the steering wheel. But yet again I was the one on the outside looking in. My plans to expose her and take Tron were ruined. Now I had no man, no baby. Happy fucking New Year to me. I got to my mother's house and immediately started drinking - shot after shot until I no longer felt the pain. As the guests started pouring in, I was finally able to peel myself off the sofa and tell my mother the news. I waited until she was in the kitchen by herself to spill the beans. "Ma..." "What's wrong with you? I saw you over there sitting all sunken in the couch. You lose your man or something?" She laughed but the comment cut me like a knife. "Donnie is pregnant." I watched and saw the color drain from her face. "She's what?" "Pregnant..." "Where is she?" "She's at home. They said they weren't coming." "They?" "Her and Tron. I went over there…she told us both at the same time." Ma looked weak, finding a seat at the kitchen table and rubbing her temples like she was getting a massive migraine. "Hey Lanesha. I wanted you to meet Bryan." Clarence came around the corner looking like the snake that he was. Since the day I caught him with my sister, he hadn't said two words to me until today. Before I could say hi to his cute friend, my mother butted in. "Donesha is pregnant." I had to laugh, Clarence looked like he'd seen a ghost. He fumbled over his words trying to get his thoughts together. "Ummm…wow…ummm…" "FIVE MINUTES UNTIL THE NEW YEAR!" someone yelled as Clarence stumbled over his words. I was tired of holding secrets and being the one getting shitted on. "Wow, that's awesome. I guess were going to be grandparents." Clarence cracked a fake smile and I had enough. "You want a drink?" Bryan asked as I stepped away. "No…I want to get out of here…" I told him honestly, walking away. As I made my way back to the living room I heard keys jingle. "My car is outside. I'm sober…where do you want to go?" He was fine, a short faded cut and deep brown skin with sparking white teeth that shone at me. His cologne was intoxicating and right now I wanted to be anywhere but here. "Wherever...you lead the way," I told him and he took my hand leading me out of the party into the cold. His car was nice, leather seats that warmed up seconds after he started the engine. "Is this a Benz?" "Yep." he said revving the engine. "And your name is Bryan?" "Yeah...a friend of Clarence." I normally wouldn't have trusted anyone that knew Clarence, but I had a good feeling about this guy. "So where are we going?" He smiled when I asked that. "Just trust me...we're going to make this night magical." I did as he said, sitting back as he turned on the radio and sped out of my mother's subdivision. I wanted the new year to mean a new life for me. No more Tron, no more Donesha, and no more settling. This year it would be all about me.

Chapter Seven

Clarence

It was the new year but I wasn't shit happy about it. I had to act like I was happy that Donesha was pregnant but on the inside I was beyond mad. But I kept it cool, especially when I saw Bryan leaving with Lonnie. At least a part of my plan was going right. Waking up New Year's Day, my wife did what she did best, and that was hit the sales. She was up and out of the house before noon and that gave me my opportunity to investigate the truth. I had to hear it from Donesha's mouth, look her in the eye and see what was really happening. I waited outside their house for Tron to leave. If I knew nothing else, he was a workaholic and getting to the dealership on New Year's Day was prime buying time. Sure enough, within an hour I saw his car backing out of the garage. I waited until he was gone off the block before I went up to the door. Knocking and ringing the bell she opened up like she was surprised to see me. "Hey...what are you doing here?" She looked around on the street. "He's gone, I saw him leave. I need to talk to you." I didn't wait to be invited in, just strolled right past her. "Clarence you can't be doing this. You can't just pop up..." "Is it true?" "Is what true?" "Don't play dumb. Are you pregnant?" She looked down and whispered so low I could barely hear her. "What?" "I said yes," she said, finally picking her head back up. "Is it mine?" Donesha had no answer to that. "It's a simple question yes or no." "I don't know okay...just leave me alone." "You need to get an abortion." "A what? Clarence get the fuck out of my house. I'm not aborting my baby." "But what if it's mine...what will that do with me and your mom and the money..." "What money?" she demanded. I had said too much. I tried to back track but it was too late. "What are you talking about Clarence. What money?" I couldn't tell her about the inheritance. The shit wasn't final yet or something that Yvette told me. It hadn't even been a year yet and I knew these things took time. "Don't change the subject. You can't do this messy shit, you hear me." I took a step towards her. "Now get rid of it. I'll give you the money." She looked at me like I had six eyes. "I want you out of my house… now!" "Bitch I'm not going nowhere. You know that's probably my baby." I was ready to hit her, make her have a miscarriage if she wasn't willing to do what the fuck I was telling her. It was a lot of money on the line and I wasn't losing it over her ass. "Bitch? Who you calling a bitch?" She backed away as I kept walking towards her. "What if I told my mama about what the fuck we've been doing." I took another step closer, looking her dead in her eyes. "You tell your Mama and I'm gonna kill you and that baby." The terror in her eyes was familiar. She looked just like Yvette right now. "Yeah your Mama looks at me the same way when I beat her ass. You wanna be next?" "What? Get the fuck out!" She ran towards the kitchen and I heard a drawer open but I didn't give a fuck about her grabbing a knife. "Come here bitch…" As I made my way to the kitchen, I heard the garage. "That's Tron. He just went out to the store, now he's back. You better get out of here before I have him fuck you up." "This ain't over." I wanted to stay, fight him and kill her but that would have to be done another day. Instead I ran out the patio door. In the back yard I walked around to the side and jumped the fence heading to my car like nothing happened. I had too much money on the line and too many bills to pay to be fucking with this young broad. Should have kept your dick in your pants. That was always my problem but I had to secure my future. These bitches weren't going to worry me. I had to deal with this issue and if she wasn't going to listen to me, then I had to get someone that would make her listen. Driving away I took out my phone and called the one person that could persuade anybody. My brother Bryan.

Chapter Eight

Bryan

Bryan jerked awake, sitting straight up in the bed. He tried to readjust his sight for a moment, not knowing whether he was in a gun fight or a shallow grave. All of those things were possibilities in his line of work but everything made sense when he saw her. Sleeping peacefully beside him was Lanesha, her face relaxed and serene as she slept naked, wrapped in his legs with a sheet haphazardly strewn across her body. His phone buzzed on the nightstand, calling for his attention. Slipping out of bed like a stealth ninja, Bryan made his way to the bathroom to take the call. "Hello…" "What happened?" Clarence asked sounding frantic. "What do you mean?" "Did you see if she knew anything?" "These things take time. I can't find all of that out in one night." Clarence made a grunt of frustration from his end of the line. "I need this to not be a situation. I need you to find this out for me." If this were a regular client, Bryan would have hung up the phone but it was Clarence, someone Bryan considered to be family so he took a deep breath and tried to stay calm. "Listen, I'll let you know in a few days what's going on." "That's not good enough." Standing in his bathroom in briefs and a bare chest he wanted to be back in bed with the warm soft body, not arguing with this old man. "C...let me do my job man," he whispered. "I got this." "You better." Without another word, Clarence hung up leaving Bryan staring at the phone. He hated disrespect and killed people for far less offense. Breathe Bryan...breathe…" he told himself, rinsing his face with cold water. He left the bathroom and went back into his master suite. He watched Lanesha sleeping like a baby for a few moments, thinking about their night together, how it was the most fun that he had in years. They laughed, danced, and partied till the wee hours of the morning. Too tired to go home they decided to go back to his place where a love making session for the ages ensued. They came together as one as if they had been together for years. Lanesha had been so gentle, rubbing him and massaging his aching muscles. Kissing and caressing him and she wasn't afraid to go down on him first without being asked. He was surprised and excited about entering her like it was his first time being with a woman. Now he crept around the room looking for her purse. Finding it under a pile of discarded clothes he went through it as quietly as he could so as not to disturb Sleeping Beauty. Nothing in the purse was interesting until he went through her phone. Going through her text messages there was one person in particular that had been texting her all night long. Answer me. Hello So you're going to ignore me We need to talk Happy New Year I guess So you're really not going to answer !!!!!! And the texts went on and on from a person that was in her phone as nothing other than T. Who the fuck is T? He didn't know, but a bit of jealousy rose in his throat. What the fuck is wrong with me? Before he could answer she began to stir in the bed, sending him to put her purse back where he found it, along with her phone, and slip back into bed right as she peeked open her eyes. "Happy New Year," she said smiling with her eyes sparkling. "Happy New Year to you beautiful." He told her pulling her close. "I had a great time last night." It was the truth, this part of him wasn't a part of the job he was working on. She laughed wrapping her arms around him. "Me too. You know I don't usually get down like this," she told him. "I'm glad you did this time." Their lips touched and tongues wrestled til the chiming sound of her phone entered the air. "Ugh...I'm so tired of that damn phone." "Then leave it. You want to go get something to eat?" "Yeah, can I take a shower here first?" "Sure...go right ahead." Damn, a girl that wants to shower first. Bryan said to himself as he watched Lanesha's sultry stroll to the bathroom. "I won't be long." She winked at him retreating to the bathroom. As soon as he heard the shower running and the sound of her stepping inside, Bryan dove for her phone. Looking through it, it was the same number, the T person was texting again. I can't believe you won't answer me. But Bryan could believe it. He listened to her hum, a soft melody filling his space where silence and loneliness usually consumed him. It felt good to have someone else around, especially a female that was so easy going and cool to be around. I know this is a job but I like her, he reasoned with himself. Stuffing the phone back into her purse he made a decision. Waiting for his house guest to finally get out of the shower, she soon emerged in a towel with her body glistening and damp. "So, where can we go eat?" Bryan shrugged, he had only one question on his mind. "You...you don't have a boyfriend or anything do you?" Lanesha was totally honest. Taking a deep breath and smiling to keep from crying she gave him the truth. "I was with someone but it was complicated. Now I'm done with him," she reasoned and that was all that Bryan needed to hear. He was the king of complicated so he could understand. "And you're done for sure?" "Yes...why you got someone in mind for me?" She asked letting her towel fall to the floor. "I might have someone in mind," he said, rising from the bed and going to the Nubian goddess in the doorway. He wanted to devour her, keep her all to himself, but for right now he would settle for bringing her into his bed. But Bryan knew he had found something special. Now he just had to figure out how to keep her from harm's way.

Months Later

Chapter Nine

Yvette

New year, new me, but I was still up to the same old things. I hadn't stopped seeing Tron and I had no plans to. I didn't give a damn that my daughter was pregnant with his baby, just like she didn't give a damn about fucking my husband in my house. In the lawyer's office I tried sitting up and being professional, but I was sending dirty text messages to Tron. I wanna eat your ass til you scream he told me, with licky emoji for added effect. Being with him made me laugh and it was fun. Fucking him earlier today in a hotel room still wasn't enough for me. I needed to see him more and the further Donesha got in her pregnancy the harder it was for him to get away. "When you gonna do that?" I texted back. "Right now...where you at?" I had to laugh. These young boys had sexual appetites that wouldn't quit. "I'm at the lawyer's office." "You still going to be able to give me that?" He asked and that was the only downside. Giving him five to ten thousand dollars every month was draining the small amount of money I was able to access of my inheritance. I was about to tell him no when the lawyer appeared. "Can I get you a water Ms. Hollins?" I was a little parched from sucking dick in the hotel and getting rabbit fucked by a boy half my age. I felt like I was back in high school skipping school while the girls were in daycare so I could pay some bills. "Yes… actually I could use some water thanks." "Alright. Be right back." I thought about my mother.. How she thought of me and my girls before she left this world. It was probably the only time she thought about us because when she was here the way she treated me took years of therapy to untangle. "Alright here is your water." My lawyer, Mr. Abitol, was the best but I guess fancy glass bottles of water was why I paid him one hundred dollars an hour. "Will your husband be in? He's not on the trust is he…?" Mr. Abitol asked and it sounded like a damn joke. Clarence wasn't going to know anything about this. I almost spit the water out onto the desk. "No sir… Just me." Mama would have never allowed that. She didn't trust a man further than she could throw them.

She asked me once, did I have a savings account of my own? When I told her I didn't believe in having money separate from my husband she damn near cursed me out. "Little girl...turn off your damn heart and turn on your brain." Mama told me that so many times it was like I had it tattooed on me. It was her mantra, the mission statement of how we lived for so many years. Driving home I thought about my Mama. The way she turned her lip up when she was mad, how she could flip anything around, and how, over all of that, she was the sneakiest bitch I knew. "What do you think of me, Mama, huh?" I imagined she could see me and was shaking her head at all the sick moves I was making. "It's you...it's all you're fucking fault I'm like this." I remembered the things I had witnessed my mother do. "Remember that time you fucked the landlord for the rent money? You did him and he came out of the room drunk and tried to lay with me....You remember that?" I remembered his stank, beer laden breath in my face when my eyes popped open. "Shhh..." he said but I screamed, running from the room, only to meet my Mama at the door. "Girl what's wrong with you." He came out scared, grabbing his clothes and limping from me kicking him in the dick for blocking my way. "You remember what you told me when he left?" She probably wouldn't, but it took me two years of counseling to get over what she told me. "I could have got my damn rent paid up through Christmas if you would have let him take a little dip...damn girl you're so fucking bougie." That was back when she smoked skinny Virginia Slims. She smoked the damn thing hard like a joint and blew the smoke in my face. That's when I figured out that using my pussy to get what I wanted wasn't just acceptable, it was expected. A year later, I was pregnant with the twins. Some guy from the neighborhood that promised riches and ghetto dreams up until I told him I was pregnant. He disappeared without a trace, then his body was found in the river with his face blown off. I felt like my life had ended. Fifteen with two babies and my Mama didn't make my life any easier. Busting into my bedroom one morning yelling at me to get up. "Look, you done had them babies. You gotta get yo ass up and get a job." "But mama what about school?" "Fuck that school shit. If you can't do that and hold down a job then you better sell some ass or something." I didn't sell myself but I knew I had to get the hell out of my mother's house. I did what I had to survive through that. And when mother got saved when I was eighteen, I left the girls with her while I went out of state and worked. I sent money back and did all I could for those girls. I didn't want them growing up like me and I realized that shit happened while they lived with my mother, but I'm sure they never woke up with a half drunk man in their bed. As I rode to the lawyer's office I thought about all of that. How I did some things just to get the bills paid while they grew up and for that little bitch to go behind my back and fuck my husband. The thought hurt me at first, it tore my heart into a million pieces. But nothing hurt my heart worse than my mother telling me to fuck the landlord at fourteen for free rent. That broke my heart, everything after that was child's play. "It's okay Mama...you warned me about her. You told me that she would be my problem child." It was true that's what Mama always told me but what would make my daughter turn on me. "Mrs. Hollins...are you okay?" I snapped out of my day dream back to the lawyer's office. "Yes...sorry. Just my thoughts getting away from me." "Well, I just wanted to let you know we were able to get a larger settlement on your mother's home. It looks like you and your daughters will get three hundred and forty two thousand instead of the amount I told you before." My mind started to swim. "What? Say that again." He repeated himself word for word. "We will have to subtract the loans you have taken against your portion, but that still leaves you with a very substantial amount." I tried to stand but my knees shook, my head started to pound. "Are you okay…?" I heard him say it but I couldn't move my mouth to tell him no. Everything started to spin until there was nothing but darkness. "Ms. Hollins… Ms. Hollins?" I heard someone calling my name but all of it felt so far away. I tried fighting through the clouds at this bright shining light. "Ms. Hollins, Ms. Hollins?" The more they called my name, the faster I ran until the light was so bright and eventually I began to see again. "There you are. Are you okay?" Mr. Albitol was right in front of me with a few other faces I didn't know. "Yes…I'm fine. What happened?" Sitting up I noticed I was on the floor. Not in chair, not on a couch but my ass was flat on the floor. "You passed out. I think it was the good news that I told you." He laughed, but I was terrified. Passing out wasn't normal, no matter how much money I was supposed to get. "Lord. I'm so embarrassed." Getting up slowly, I felt like the whole staff was packed into the little office. "How long was I out?" "Maybe about a minute or two. Wasn't even long enough for us to call an ambulance." "I am so sorry Mr. Albitol. I am so embarrassed."I wished I could have run out of the office, but my legs still felt like putty. "Is there anyone for you to call?" I tried to think fast but Clarence was out of town again. Even if he was in town, he wouldn't be a viable option. I didn't want to see Donesha; since the new year I hadn't even laid eyes on her. Just text messages and faking being busy made it easy for us to stay out of each other's way. Little bitch was probably feeling guilty so she stayed out of my way. My mind went into that situation and before I knew, it Mr. Albitol was calling me back. "You sure you are okay, Yvette?" I wasn't sure how to answer that. Mama used to have dizzy spells, then she found out it was heart failure. Am I getting sick? Maybe it was time for me to see a cardiologist and make sure I wasn't at risk for anything hereditary. I put it off so long and now here I was passing out in my lawyer's office. "Is there no one we can call to pick you up?" Mr. Albitol asked and I could only think of one person. The only other man I could trust. "Yeah I have someone. But tell me. When can I get the money?" "All you have to do is sign these papers and we can have the accounts all set up for you and your girls." It was that easy. "Fine. Let's do that now and I'll make a call for my ride," I told him. "Get Mrs. Hollins the papers please," he said to a member of his staff. They went running the instant he gave the orders, and putting the phone to my ear I prayed that he would answer. Sure enough, on the third ring I heard his voice. "Hello…" "Tron, its Yvette. I need your help." He was the only person I could call right now.

Chapter Ten

Iron

I fucked her this morning and now here we were still together this afternoon doing what she wanted. Was I her fucking stool pigeon or something? She had my nuts in a vice, whether it was for sex or for an errand, when Yvette called I had to go running...at least for now. But today we drove in silence. She hadn't said a word since she got in the car. She was gazing out the window as if I wasn't even here. When we finally were within blocks of the house she blurted out questions. "How is my daughter?" Yvette asked. "Getting big. She's almost six months now." "God it's been that long." "Yeah we're almost at June." "Jeez…" She shook her head as I pulled into her driveway. "Has she said anything about me or does she know anything about this?" she asked pointing from me to her and back again. "Naw, she's just been focused on school and the baby's room. She said she just didn't want any negativity in the new year so she doesn't want to see you." For some reason that gave Yvette a hysterical laugh. "She doesn't want the negativity of me? That's hilarious." She laughed as I pulled into her driveway. "Isn't that a bitch?" "What?" She jumped from the car going to the porch like her ass was on fire. "God dammit…" On the porch she walked back and forth cursing and stomping like a toddler. "What the hell is it?" I yelled, getting out of the car. "My chairs. They're gone. Someone is fucking with my porch again." She stomped around then she staggered a bit. "Whoa…" I caught her, grabbing her before she fell. "You have to take it easy," I told her, but there was no calming Yvette down. "Fuck that. I got the cameras now. I'm going to see who the hell this is." She staggered into the house, flopping down on the sofa. "Are you okay." "Why?" "You look flushed." "Yeah I'm great. Actually never been better," she said, her eyes in her phone. I watched her, how she seemed tired her eyes drooping as she tried working through the app. "You seemed tired earlier today too." "You trying to say you didn't have a good time with me?" she asked as I frantically shook my head. "No, that's not what I mean I was just saying that…"

"Oh my fucking God." "What?" "That bitch. I should have known it had something to do with his lying ass." She flipped the screen of the phone over so I could see. "What the hell is that?" I asked. "Clarence's ex-wife." "Ex-wife? What the fuck is she doing here?" "I don't know, but I'm done. I'm done with his ass." "You're kicking him out?" "Yeah I've had it with his shit. The cheating bastard fucking my..." She stopped herself. "Fucking with my life. I'm just done. Plus I got good news today," she said standing up slowly. "What's that then?" "I'm getting the inheritance. I'm going to tell the girls soon and they'll know." "Oh yeah..." "And guess what, I'm getting back way more than I thought we were." That sent my mind dancing. I needed money. I was about to be a father and had bills to pay off. I barely scraped by and paid Donesha's tuition payment. "So you're going to tell them soon?" "When everything is finalized I will," she said, walking towards the stairs. "Where are you going now?" "To pack my husband's shit. You should leave. Thanks for giving me a ride home." She seemed different right now, more focused and almost angry. "You sure you're okay?" "Hell yeah, I'm fine. I just have shit to do. Life isn't getting any slower and I'm not getting any younger. Time to get this trash out of my way," she said taking to the stairs. I watched her as she climbed up the steps and disappeared at the top. Just to think, earlier today we were fucking and now she was about to get rid of her husband and she just told me that my girl was going to get three hundred thousand dollars. "Alright I'm gone then…" "Thanks. Lock the bottom lock when you leave." That was it. I was outside, headed towards my car. I counted bills in my head as I drove. Leaving Yvette's house behind I tried to think of everything I had to pay when I got a call. "Hello?" "So you dodging me now?" The number was unfamiliar but I would know the voice anywhere. "Oh wassup Melo?" "You heard my question or you just going to play like you didn't hear?" "Naw man I'm not dodging you." "It feels like it nigga. Where is my payment?" I thought quick, trying to find a good excuse. "Ummm man…" "Umm my ass. Time is up nigga." Melo didn't scream or raise his voice. It was more like a promise and less like a threat but all the same, I heard a click and then a long silence. "What? What does that mean?" The line was dead, I might as well have been talking to myself. "FUCK!" I punched the steering wheel. Waiting at a red light I thought about calling him back. Maybe I could explain or get him some money for the moment until all this inheritance shit became clear. Looking at my phone, I debated on calling him back when I heard screeching tires. I couldn't turn around fast enough to see before the flash of a black car came speeding right up beside me. I couldn't move or react when I saw the gun pointing out the window. All I had time to do was close my eyes. I heard the sound of the windows breaking and my skin felt like it was on fire.

Chapter Eleven

Donesha

"So what brings you in today?" Same me but new therapist all these years later. I would have been fine if it wasn't for Clarence. Now I was a few months removed from that day and I still couldn't stop thinking about it. "I'm having nightmares. I'm really afraid of someone." "Oh…do tell." She took out a notepad scribbling notes as I spilled all of my secrets. I breezed through everything letting it out like some long run on sentence. "Wow…" she said as I finally finished. Readjusting her bun and cleaning her glasses, I could tell she was stalling for time to put everything together. "I have a complicated life." It was the truth, there was nothing simple about me. Everything relationship that I had was strained in some sort of way.

"Yeah it is. Do you feel that this man will harm you? You say his name is Clarence." I had no idea, thinking about that day scared me and all I could do was shrug it off to keep from crying. "So you aren't afraid?" "Oh I am. But what can I do about it?" She couldn't answer because there was no answer to this craziness. I had gotten myself into this I was going to have to figure a way out. "I want to say if you do feel like you are in danger, maybe it would be a good time to talk to your mother." I wanted to slap her for even suggesting that. "What would that do?" "Coming clean to her and letting her know about the threat will give you an ally to help and…" "I told you, he said he hits her too. What the hell is she going to do?" She took a deep breath sitting back in her own chair. "I'm sorry I misspoke. I forgot about that part." She shook her head for a moment then sat in silence. "It's just going to be messed up either way. But I'll get through it. Thanks for your time." This wasn't like when I was in undergrad. Back then I thought molestation and abandonment were the worst things that could happen to you, but I was wrong. Being pregnant and your mother's abusive husband potentially being the father is by far the worst thing. I stood to leave, making it to the door before she could say a word. I stopped listening anyway as she called my name a few times to come back. I was halfway to my car about to break down in tears as I waddled my pregnant self to the parking lot when my phone began to ring. "Yeah." I assumed it was the therapist begging me to come back but instead a man's voice filled the phone. "Hello. May I speak to Donesha Hill please?" "Speaking." "This is Sergeant Craters from the Metropolitan police department." My heart stopped beating as I thought about what could of been wrong or what I did wrong. "Yes." "There was an accident involving Trontavious Carter. We need you down to the hospital right away." "Are you serious?" "Yes ma'am. Very serious. How quickly can you be here?" Five minutes ago I was trying to figure out my life and now everything in my life stood still. I didn't know whether to cry or to breakdown, but I needed help. "I'll be right there." With shaking hands I hung up the phone and out of instinct I dialed her number, my hands were working on their own as the phone began to ring. I don't know if it's been guilt or shame that's made me unable to face her, but right now I needed her. "Hello..." "Mom..." The tears came before I could get it out. "Tron's been in an accident. I'm at the school and I need to get to him. I'm so nervous I can't drive." "I'm on my way," was all that she said. No questions, no excuses, she was just on her way. God forgive me for what I've done. I asked the stars as I rubbed my belly. Please don't let this be Clarence's baby. If it was I would never be able to forgive myself and neither would my mother.

Chapter Twelve

Eve

Dressed in black from the top of her hoodie to the bottom of her sneakers Eve was good at blending in and going unnoticed. In the dark of night, she was able to get to the side of the house admiring the beauty of the huge home that her baby daddy shared with his woman. "So this is the house that you bought for her?" Eve asked the air, because no one was around to answer. The house looked huge from the outside, a two car garage, two stories as far as she could see with a huge backyard. "Our daughter could have played in that yard," she said while making her way to the backyard. Peeking through the patio window she didn't see anyone home but what she did see made her head pound. "A fucking marble countertop. Glass chandelier, a huge granite top kitchen table." She ogled over all of the details of the house. And the more she saw the more pissed off she became with the man she spent a couple of years serving as his on call sex partner. "You tell me that you love me. Then you buy this bitch a house." Two large plastic trash containers sat on the porch with trash overflowing from it. "What do we have here? Evidence of how horrible of a father you are? How you neglected me and your daughter when we needed you most?" Armed with latex gloves and a flashlight Eve looked through the trash, picking through bags like a dirty raccoon. She didn't see anything of interest, just food wrappers and discarded papers, until she saw it. An order form for invitations. "What is this you planning a little party without your baby's mother?" she asked, but unfolding the order form she had to read it a good five times before it set in. "You are cordially invited to the gender reveal of our child!" Eve screamed the words shrieking in the backyard like a wounded animal. "You piece of shit. You have a baby with her, a gender reveal, and a few months ago you let my daughter die?" Eve was beyond upset as she kicked the trash cans over, spewing the contents all over the back patio. With the swiftness of a martial artist, she produced a can of lighter fluid and matches from her pocket. Dousing the porch in the flammable liquid she made sure to soak the wood particularly heavily near the house. "You built this castle, this life, now how is it going to feel to see it all go up in flames?" She lit the match, instantly sending the patio up in a huge ball of flames. Jumping from the porch, she laughed as the flames took over the wooden structure she had just been standing on. And just like she planned, the fire reached the house, sending the patio window into flames before the loud thunderous sound of glass breaking from the heat made her jump. "Oohhhh fireworks." She clapped as she watched the show. Within two minutes the entire back half of the house was engulfed and finally, she felt a bit of peace. "See if you can put your life back together now." Slipping off her gloves, with her hood up Eve jumped a few fences, taking a more scenic route through the neighbors' backyards as she heard the sound of sirens and fire trucks. By the time she made it back to the street at the end of the block, she could see the entire house was burning. The roof liked like a roasting barbecue pit of flames and she couldn't have been happier. "I'm not done yet you son of a bitch," she told the wind, pretending it was Tron. "I'm just getting started."

To Be Continued…

ALL KINDS OF
CRAZY
II

Billie Dureyea Shell

PROLOGUE

Rex and one of his goons entered the empty rent house. He'd ordered the other goon working for him to stay in the car with Moneca; who was still unconscious. They headed for the basement intending to remove City's body; whom he assumed was dead. As soon as they entered the door to the basement, the goon's leg was yanked from beneath him. He swung his arms out as he fell down the concrete stairs, knocking Rex's gun out of his hands. "Run, Oneca. Run!" City yelled as he still had a grip on the goon's leg. They began wrestling at the bottom of the stairs, both going for the gun that had slid to the corner of the room. The injured men were throwing blows to one another, desperate to be the first one to grab the gun. No matter how many times City pummeled the goon, he was relentless, and continued to retaliate hitting City with powerful force. City felt himself becoming weak, as he had already lost so much blood. He just wanted to keep fighting until he knew Oneca was safe. While the men were fighting, Rex had managed to limp his way down the stairs, heading for the gun himself. Oneca had been crouching behind the stairs watching the entire thing. As soon as she saw Rex hit the bottom of the stairs and move towards the gun, she dashed up the stairs bursting through the door. She looked back at City, who was on the ground, under the goon who was repeatedly punching him in the face. She stared at him through teary eyes. His face was covered in blood and one of his eyes was swollen shut. "Get out of here!" City yelled at her. She turned and ran just as Rex grabbed the gun pointing it towards her. She ran at full speed through the empty house, abruptly stopping when she heard a gunshot ring out from the basement. Her heart stopped as she just knew that City had been shot again. She ran out of the front door straight into the arms of the second goon who'd been waiting outside. He was making his way into the house after hearing the gun shot. "No!" she cried out as he grabbed her. She swung her arms wildly, desperately trying to escape him, but he gripped her tightly. Out of nowhere, a figure rushed them swinging wildly on the goon, hitting him in his head repeatedly. "Let her go," Moneca yelled as she desperately tried to fight the man who was twice her size. He loosened his grip on Oneca as he made an attempt to grab Moneca. Oneca was able to jerk her body away from him. "Run baby, run," Moneca yelled as the goon was now able to grab her with two hands slamming her body onto the ground. "Mama," Oneca cried out as she watched the man continue to viciously attack her mother as she laid on the ground. "Oneca, I said run," Moneca yelled again, "I mean it! Now!" Oneca turned and ran at full force down the dark street.

Chapter 1:

MIKEY

Women ain't shit. I'm tired of being the good guy. All my life I've had to take shit from other people. It all started from my father. I've had to listen to him tell me over and over about how I'm weak, powerless, frail, and won't ever amount to anything. And what do I do while he's castigating my balls? Not a damn thing! Just sit there and let him talk to me like I'm a punk. Well I, Michael Jarrod Lee, am tired of being disrespected. I've let my father, Raymond Lee aka Rex, berate me my whole life and I'll be damned if I let a woman make me feel like less of a man. I know Oneca is cheating on me. I can feel it in my gut. I just haven't been able to prove it. She just don't act the same. I'm tired of everyone thinking that I'm some kind of punk. I'm sick of being walked over. I know Oneca has problems but I never thought that she would do me wrong, especially after everything that I've been through with her. I'm so in love with the beautiful, Oneca Cheyenne Alvarez. This is the woman who I got down on one knee and asked to be my wife. The only woman I've ever loved, other than my mama of course. I would give Oneca the world, but something's not right. Yes, she went through some crazy things in her life. Yes, she learned that she had another identity, the infamous Ocean, but I didn't and still don't care. I was sent into Oneca's life under false pretenses by my father, but quickly fell in love with her beauty and innocence. It killed me every day to not be able to tell her how I really felt and that my father was obsessed with her family. I've never been anything like my father. I had no interest in pimping women or selling drugs. I'm just a low key type of guy who likes watching sports and anything that has to do with science fiction. Some might consider me a square, but I am who I am, and I've been okay with that for years. When I first saw Oneca, I couldn't believe how beautiful she was. When she looked at me with those slanted, brown eyes, I felt like the world stood still. In my eyes, she was so pure and she liked me for me. Each day that our friendship grew, I felt horrible for deceiving her, but I was slowly falling for her, and felt like I would never get the chance to tell her. After all that Oneca went through in her life, and learning of all the people who betrayed her, she still chose to keep me around. She loved me all along, just like I had loved her, and I was grateful for that. We'd been going strong for two years and I planned on asking her to be my wife. A phone call from Ocean's boyfriend, City, ruined everything. It was times like that, I wished that I had the ruthless heart of my father because if I could kill City I would have. I didn't understand why he couldn't leave her alone, I mean he was in prison for a reason, and she put him there. As far as I know, Ocean has not returned. All of the horrible events from Oneca and Moneca's past have been revealed, and they are both learning to cope with these things through therapy. Ocean was created to protect them from the terrible things that they experienced because they were not able to mentally handle them. But now that all of these things from their past have been presented to them, the need for a protector does not exist. If City is ever successful in bringing Ocean back, then I could lose Oneca forever. I have laid next to her at night, and I've heard her mention his name. I've never told her this, but I know she dreams about him. I can tell that she doesn't fear him either, it's almost like she longs for him. She won't let me make love to her but she moans in her sleep like she's giving it him. It pisses me off that she's with me and she's dreaming about this dude. I can't get the thoughts out of my mind of Oneca cheating on me. I proposed to Oneca and she accepted, but she won't pick a wedding date and I feel that she has been procrastinating. She claims that she would like to take time to get herself together and make sure that she is really okay. But I just don't know if I buy it. Oneca, her mother, and I all moved to Oklahoma City to start over. I was able to get a job with the Bank of Oklahoma and maintain my career as an account specialist. Oneca took a job at the OU Children's Hospital as an operator and eventually decided that she would like to go back to school and earn a degree in Nursing. This has taken up so much of her time and I'm starting to feel like a second thought to her. Between her attending school, her therapy sessions, and still working as an operator at night, I don't feel like I ever get to see my fiancée. I've tried to stay cool about it, but I have developed obsessive thoughts about Oneca being with another man. She doesn't know it, but three weeks ago I downloaded an application to her cell phone that allows me to track all of her whereabouts. I spy on her all the time. I follow her around and I'm just waiting on the day when I catch her ass up. I hadn't noticed anything odd about her whereabouts until today. I didn't know what the hell she was doing on the West side of the city, but this was not the first time that I'd tracked her there. I knew her classes were over for the day, but normally she would go straight home to prepare for work that night. She attended class at the University of Oklahoma in Norman which was about 20 miles south of OKC. We lived on the North side right off of Memorial road, so what the hell was she doing way out on 122nd and Council? After some time had passed I noticed that she had been at this same location for over an hour. I didn't know who the hell lived there, but my pride couldn't take it anymore. I needed to find out what was going on. I quickly made up an excuse to leave work and drove straight to the residential area.

Chapter 2

MIKEY

When I arrived I noticed her black Acura parked in the driveway along with another white SUV. I knew she was messing around on me, I could feel it. I parked down the street from the brick home making sure that I could get a good view of what was going on. I had not thought this plan out entirely as I was unsure of what to do now. I watched the home for about an hour. I called her cell phone several times and it pissed me off each time that she didn't answer. I texted her, 'Hey Babe Call me', but she didn't still didn't respond. Although I wanted to, I knew deep down that I didn't have the balls to go up to that house and confront her. Just as I was getting ready to drive away, my ringing phone startled me. "Hello?" "Is this my traitor ass son?" "What do you want pops?" I responded in an exasperated tone. "What you doing?" He asked. "Why?" I was short with him. "Damn, son! Why so hostile?" He laughed. I let out a deep breath out of frustration, "You only call when you want something, so what is it?" "Tell your crack head ass mama to stay away from my house. My wife and I are getting tired of her shit," "For real Pops? That's how you feel? It's your fault she's even strung out in the first place," "Blame who you want. You just need to get her in check. Tell her to quit coming around here begging, I aint got shit for her. And who the hell you think you talking to anyway? Nigga, I'm still your daddy," I shook my head out of frustration. If he would have stayed in Georgia, he wouldn't have to worry about my mama. "Look, I got to go," "What you doing? Worrying about that psycho ass woman of yours?" "I already told you not to ever mention Oneca again," I said. "Oh nigga, just because you got your feelings hurt the last time, don't mean I'm not gone tell it how it is. I told you she wasn't shit, but you aint shit either, so I guess it's a match made in heaven. But since you do have my blood running through you, I at least got a little sympathy for your dumb ass, so I try to offer a little advice. You think that bitch aint fucking around? She's a hoe, just like her mama," he laughed into the phone, "It runs in their family,""Oh yea, but you are the one who is married to her grandma? What kind of shit is that?" "Don't worry about what the fuck I do. Just know this; I'm always 2 steps ahead. Never underestimate Rex Lee," he laughed at himself. "Yea whatever, like I said, I'm busy," I said with disgust. "Hey watch your tone young man," he said mockingly, "Just remember what your pops told you, you'll thank me one day. I guarantee, my words will ring true," I couldn't stand the sound of his cackling for one more second, "Don't forget what I said about your mama." He said before hanging up. I wonder what God was trying to prove by giving me the life that I'd been given. Why did Rex have to be my father? Why did I have to son of a drug addicted whore and a self-centered ass pimp? The only thing that did make sense in my life was my love for Oneca, and hell, her parents were just as fucked up as mine. Movement down the street caused me to refocus my attention. I saw a tall thin Hispanic girl come out of the house. I recognized her as Oneca's friend, Camilla. I breathed a sigh of relief as I realized that I was overreacting again. My phone suddenly went off alerting me that I had a text, 'Hey baby had to stay late at class, just now headed home. Love you.' I read Oneca's lying ass text. I threw the phone on the floor of my car out of frustration, wondering why in the hell she was lying. I suddenly noticed a man exit the home followed by Oneca. I tried to study the guy from so far away. He was light skinned, tall, about 6'4", with a scruffy goatee. He had a little weight on him from what I could tell, as they were all dressed in scrubs. My baby was just smiling from ear to ear and laughing with the both of them. I watched her give the Latina girl a hug and her and the guy jumped in her car. I ducked down in my seat praying to God that she drove the other direction. After a few moments I raised in my seat. What the fuck was this nigga doing in her car? "Damn Oneca, you fucking around on me?" I said out loud to myself. "I told your dumb ass!" I heard a muffled voice exclaim. I looked around confused, then noticed my phone on the floor where I had thrown it. I picked it up noticing that my pops was still on the phone. Damn did my phone accidentally dial him? I put the phone to my ear, not knowing what to say, I felt humiliated. "I know you on here," he stated, "When you gone learn son? Daddy knows best." I hung up the phone pissed at the world.

Chapter 3:
ONECA

I glanced over at Rashaad as we rode down the highway. He sure was handsome, but nothing could compare to my baby Mikey. I couldn't wait to get home and spend a little time with him before my night shift at the hospital. Life has been going pretty well for me. I just wish Mikey wouldn't act so crazy and jealous. Ever since City called our home, my man has not been the same. I don't know what I can do to convince him that I don't want anyone, but his ass. It's becoming stressful because he is always accusing me of something. He has started making me feel constrained, like I can't be free to do what I want. He treats me exactly like my father used to treat me. He has never said it, but I think he believes that Ocean may come back around and leave a trail of destruction like she has in the past. I'm scared to tell Mikey that there are times that I still black out because I'm scared might leave me. There are times when I have missed big chunks of my days and I don't who I've been with or where I been. Everyone around me acts as if nothing is happening, so I try to act as normal as possible. But the black outs have been getting worse and worse. Working at the Children's Hospital as an operator, did cause me to gain an interest in nursing, so I made the decision to enter Nursing school a year ago. It has been going really well. I get along with all of my classmates, but I've become really close with Camilla and Rashaad. We all could relate to each other because we all wanted to go into Pediatric Nursing. Camilla's personality was the opposite of mine, she was a fireball. Her outgoing personality and beauty caused her to constantly be the center of attention. She was thin, but shapely and her beautiful dark hair flowed down her back. She did not have a Mexican accent, but would curse you out in Spanish at the drop of a dime. Rashaad was tall and handsome. He was definitely a pretty boy with his light brown skin and curly dark hair. He actually was a top Basketball player at the University of

Oklahoma, but 6 years ago a leg injury caused him to have to hang up his dreams of entering the NBA. He dropped out of school for a while, but finally decided to re-enroll at OU as a nursing student. He was definitely the class clown and was always cracking jokes. Although I'd never seen him in action, I also believed him to be a ladies man. "Oneeeca….earth to Oneca," Rashaad waved his hand in front of my face, snapping me out of my thoughts. "Oh, my bad," I said smiling. "Damn girl," he laughed, "I need you to pay attention while you driving me around, I would like to live to see 26," he joked. "Boy please, you will get home safely," I teased. "Take this next exit," he said pointing up ahead, "I appreciate you giving me a ride home, my truck should be out of the shop tomorrow," "No problem, I'm just glad we were able to get some more study time in. That test next week is going to be a beast," I sighed. "I know man, got a nigga rethinking this whole nursing thing," he said as he directed me into his apartment complex off of NW Expressway and Macarthur. "Rashaad, you make the best grades in the class, don't play," "I know, I do, don't I?" He said rubbing his goatee in a cocky way. "Boy get out of my car," I laughed while parking in an open space. "Yea, we wouldn't want your man to come jumping out the bushes," he joked. I smiled, although I know Rashaad was only joking, he just didn't know how crazy Mikey had been acting lately. "Aww shit. Did I hit a nerve?" he asked noticing that I didn't laugh at his joke. "Naw, me and my boo are good," I replied quickly. "As good as you look, I would hide in the bushes any day." he laughed opening the door and getting out. I didn't know what to say, he had never complimented me like that before. I watched him unlock his door and turn around and wave to me. I didn't want to let Rashaad know, but his joke had hit a nerve. I didn't think Mikey was bold enough to hide in bushes, but he definitely would not have liked the fact that I gave Rashaad a ride home. Lately, he didn't like anything that I did that didn't involve him. That's why I lied and told him I had to stay at school late. A couple of weeks ago Camilla and I went and got something to eat after class. Mikey lost his damn mind when I didn't show up at home at my usual time. He started flipping out and accusing me of cheating on him. I hate lying to him, but it was just easier that way. He is just so insecure and I can't stand it. I try to cut him some slack because I know he catches a lot of hell from his father for being with me. His father hates my family, which is ironic because we should have a hit out on him for all the bullshit he has put my family through. I wish Mikey would learn how to stand up to his father. I can't stand to see him and his father interact with each other. Mikey resorts to being this meek little boy and his father is an asshole. To add even more drama to the mix, my grandmother, Wynita, is married to Mikey's father Rex. My mother, Moneca, and I haven't spoken to her in a long time because she decided to stay married to Rex even after she learned all of the horrible things he did to my mother. How in the hell can you stay married to a man who used to be with your daughter in the first place? On top of that he had her raped, beat the shit out of her, raped again, and then was the reason behind her being held in a psychiatric facility against her will. I know my grandma didn't have the easiest life either, but that's no excuse. According to my mother, when her husband left her she completely lost it. She went into some sort of depressive lethargic state for years. My mother thinks that losing another man would probably kill her so she tries not to take it personal. I, personally, take it really personal. You would think I would let family betrayal roll off my back. A little over two years ago I learned that my father, well the man that raised me, sexually abused me as a child. His excuse was that it wasn't me, but only Ocean during all of the intimate encounters. My other identity, Ocean, did in fact protect me during the abuse, and I was never aware of what was going on. This man raised me by himself and I adored him. Growing up without a mother, I did have moments where I felt incomplete, but my father was able to make me feel more than loved. When the abuse was revealed, it was too much for me to handle. It took some time for me to be able to process what was being told to me. Dr. Green recommended, Dr. Barnett, a psychiatrist here in Oklahoma City that I could see on a weekly basis. Dr. Barnett is great and has really helped me work through the memories of abuse that sporadically come to me. It all started to make sense on why I was never comfortable with my sexuality, and even to this day, I have not been able to make love with Mikey. I was forced to make a hard decision when I had to testify against my father and he was ultimately sentenced to 20 years in prison. I haven't seen or heard from him since. I wondered if Mikey was even home as I pulled into our apartment complex because I did not see his car. I parked and grabbed my things hurrying inside. The house was dark as I walked in. I walked into the bedroom and screamed out as I noticed a dark figure sitting on the bed. I ran back to the door, "Get your ass up!" I yelled to the intruder as I grabbed a knife off the kitchen bar. The figure did not move, but just sat there looking at me. Confused I flipped on the bedroom light. "Mikey! What the hell are you doing! Why are you playing? Sitting in here in the dark," "Why did you do it?" He said in a low voice. "Do what? What is wrong with you?" I exclaimed. "You fucking around on me? Is that why you won't let me make love to you?" He accused. "Mikey are you serious?" "Just answer the damn question!" His voice rose, but he remained on the bed. "Mikey, baby I don't know what you are talking about," I said moving closer to him. I was shocked to see that his eyes were bloodshot, "Baby have you been drinking?" my question was immediately answered as I caught a whiff of the alcohol on his breath. "Hell yea I've been drinking," he spit, "My fiancée is a fucking whore," I was so taken aback by his words that I was speechless. "You aint shit," he glared at me. "Why are you talking to me like that?" I could feel the tears on the rims of my eyelids. "Why don't you ask that nigga you were with today?" It suddenly hit me, he must have seen me with Rashaad today, "Baby it's not what you think, I swear. Rashaad is in my study group," "I don't give a damn," he yelled, quickly standing up, "You nothing, but a slut just like your damn mama!" "What!" I said out of shock. Mikey had never spoken to me like this before. "You heard me," he spit. "Mikey how could you say that about my mother? You know what happened to her?" by now the tears were flowing. "Your mama was a hoe way before that, Oneca, don't try to flip this around. I saw your ass with him today," "I just gave him a ride! His truck is in the shop! We were at Camilla's studying," I exclaimed. "And to think, I wanted you to be my wife," he turned his nose up as he stumbled into the bathroom. By now, I was furious. I quickly took the ring off throwing it at the back of his head, "Take your ring! You asshole! I can't believe you talking to me like that," "Take your ass out of here," he yelled. "Oh, I'm going to work, you bastard!" I slammed the door as I left our apartment.

I sat in my car for several minutes trying to fight back more tears. He didn›t even bother to come running after me. I just don›t know what has gotten into him. I love Mikey, I really do, but he›s a fool if he thinks he can get away with talking to me like that. I was glad he didn›t run after me because after I thought about what he said about my mother, I couldn›t even stand the sight of him. I hoped that work would be busy tonight to keep my mind occupied. Working the 3-11 shift was tough at times and I know it has placed a lot of strain on my relationship with Mikey, but I was determined to earn my degree in nursing and this shift worked with my class schedule. With Mikey working 6-2 at the bank, we rarely saw each other. I just didn›t know how much longer we could go on like this. I'd been at work a couple of hours when my cell started ringing from an unidentified number. "Hello?" "Oneca, its Rashaad" "Oh, hey Rashaad," I said flatly. "Damn, did I catch you at a bad time?" "No, it's just been a long day. What's up?" "I think I left my phone in your car, I can't find it anywhere. I'm using my neighbor's phone right now, you think you can bring it by?" "I guess I can, but I don't get off work until 11 tonight," "That's cool, I'll be looking for you." By the time my shift ended, I was more upset then when I went in to work. Mikey hadn't bothered to call or text me at all. I couldn't believe how irrational he was being. I wanted to call my mother and vent to her, but I didn't want her to worry about me and Mikey's relationship. Lately, he was accusing me of cheating all the time, but this time was definitely the worse. If I told her about every little time, then she would just worry. I pulled into Rashaad's apartment complex right before midnight. I grabbed his cellphone and hopped out of my car. He opened the door before I could even knock. "I heard you coming up the stairs," he grinned. "Oh, okay," I laughed. "Come in," he opened the door. "I can't stay, just wanted to bring your phone," I said stepping inside. The apartment was dimly lit. There was a flat screen mounted on the wall, and Sports Center was on the screen, muted. "Something smells good," I commented taking a seat on the couch. I watched him rush into his small kitchen, "Damn, I forgot about my garlic bread," he said opening his oven. "Let me find out you're Mr. Chef Boyardee," I joked. He walked back into the living room, grinning from ear to ear, which made his dimples deepen even more. "Girl, you better ask somebody. I puts it down," he took a seat next to me on the couch, "I'm a night owl, I always cook late. Tonight, I made Chicken Alfredo. You want some?" "No, I gotta get home," I said looking down at my cell phone that was in my hands. "You sure you're alright?" he asked with concern. I shook my head yes then quickly shook it no, "Mikey and I had a fight," I said looking at my cell phone again. I just couldn't get over how he hadn't called, and by now he knew I was off of work. "Aww shit," he replied, "Are ya'll good?" "I don't know, Rashaad. He said some messed up stuff," I tried to hold back, but my eyes watered up. "It's going to be okay," he said as his thumb caught the first tear that fell from my eye. The pleasure that I felt from his affection suddenly caused me to feel really uncomfortable. Prior to Mikey, I had no experience with a man and was flat out a prude when it came to the opposite sex. I mean, there was that one time with City, but I definitely wouldn't consider myself experienced. Mikey and I hadn't even had sex yet, I just wasn't ready, and appreciated that he was willing to wait. Even after he confessed his love for me, I just wasn't psychologically ready. And now, I knew that it all was related to the sexual abuse by my father. Mikey definitely moved at a slower pace than most men. Somehow, I didn't get that vibe from Rashaad. I leaned back away from him, as I wiped my eyes, "Umm, I should probably go," I stated. He looked at me with concern, "I don't want you to feel uncomfortable, but you are clearly upset," "I am, but me being here with you can't do anything, but make it worse," I said standing up. Rashaad stood up with me, "Okay, I understand. You sure you don't want me to make you a plate to go?" Before I could object, my phone started to vibrate in my hand, I quickly checked the message. 'You might as well move your shit to his house slut. I see everything' My heart stopped. How in the hell did Mikey know I was here? "Oh no!" I began to panic. "What? What's wrong?" Rashaad asked alarmed. "He knows I'm here," I collapsed back on the couch. "Damn, what he got, GPS tracker on you?" Rashaad was shocked. "Do you mind if I use your bedroom? I need to call him?" I asked already making my way into his bedroom. I shut the door and quickly called Mikey's phone. I became frustrated as he kept sending me to voicemail. 'PICK UP' I hurriedly pressed send on my text. I was beginning to get pissed off. I decided that I needed to go home and handle this in person. "Rashaad, I'm headed home," I said as I quickly exited his bedroom and headed for the front door. "Everything cool?" he asked from the kitchen. "Nothing I can't handle," I smiled as waved bye to him. "Call me if you need to." he called out as I shut his door and rushed to my car. When I made it home, it didn't take me long to realize that Mikey was not there. I continued to call his cell phone, but his phone was turned off. I could not believe he was acting this way. 'Please call me. I LOVE YOU.' I sent my final text before climbing into bed and crying myself to sleep.

CONFLICTED

Billie Dureyea Shell

Chapter 1

Sitting upright and confident in a park chair opposite a wooden chess board, Detective Sensi Mendez faced his amateur opponent wearing a self-assured, smug grin. He sat comfortably under a lamp-post near a large oak tree at the far side of the Hackney Downs Community Park in East London, which gave him a complete view of the bustling high street ahead whilst he was hidden by the trees branches and autumn coloured leaves. "You planning on telling me what›s on your mind, or you gonna stay eyeballing the board to catch my move?» The detective's young and undefeated challenger asked, seeing the detective's impatience while he studied the board to make a move. He took his eyes off the board for a brief moment before finally administrating his move. "Play, son." The Detective said, looking up at his opponent and gesturing for him to make a move. He then pulled a cigar out the inside pocket of his trench coat, and popped it into his mouth letting it droop slightly. "Don't worry about me old man, I got this," the young man replied as he leaned back in his chair full of attitude. He gave Sensi his undivided attention and waited patiently for what the detective had to say. "What makes you think I called you for anything else other than a friendly game? You know I very rarely like to mix business with our time." Sensi said stealing a move within the blink of his opponent's eyes. 'Our time?" His opponent turned up his nose at the thought. 'This nigga wants something, I can tell.' "Because I know you, you play dirty even when you're playing against your own, but it's all good." The young man said studying the board. "This is my game, and there ain't anything you can do to throw me off it. I'm about to take your knight out." He laughed out loud and pointed at the playing board. Sensi had arranged what was left of his playing pieces till they were scattered across the board, though there was a single knight protecting two pawns and a bishop. "You need to stop protecting these little nigga's and stay focused on your queen, cause if she gets knocked... its game over." The young man continued whilst anticipating his next move. "In chess, yes, you're correct." Sensi said. "But out here you're so wrong." He chimed before lighting his cigar and exhaling the smoke in the opposite direction. "It's like this, try to think of your queen as your woman or, how do you youngster's say it? You're wifey or boo." The middle-aged detective laughed, mocking the words the youngsters used in the streets today. "Naturally you're the King and the board is your domain." He coughed, and took his time catching his breath before he wheezed on. "Most of you youngen's spend your time chasing one bitch." He cackled, then spat on the ground. "Now that I think about it, you're all out here chasing the same bitch." He coughed again, spitting out some saliva while wiping his mouth with the end of his hand then motioning to his opponent to make his move. Detective Sensi and his opponent, Essen Boaten, comically bantered over their futile c'hess game, the rules of the streets, and the lifestyle they often called 'the game.' Both men played exceptionally well, but it was neither to win nor lose. They played to strategize their position in the game, playing out their lives on the board. "See, there you go getting me mixed up with your son. I know for a fact you ain›t tryna put me in that category. When have you ever seen me chasing a bitch? Let alone a bitch some other pricks' claiming," Essen snapped. He shook his head, and moved his bishop taking one of the detective's pawns out of the game. "Power is your bitch, Essen." The detective said raising his voice. "Power and respect, and that skirt you and Judas are chasing is the lifestyle that comes with her. I've seen so many little nigga's in my time, just like you and Judas, trying to juggle them all and fail. Like two out of the three ain't enough. But that's why I put you down young man, because nobody smells your bitch. I see her, but I ain't smelt her yet." Sensi said puffing once and coughing twice. He laughed. "Take a good look at the board son, your queen is defenseless without you, yet she is the alpha and omega of the game. You own her world yet you're at her command. Show a bit of love to your other players once in a while, and they got just as much to lose as you do, if not more." "You're going mental Mr. M." Essen laughed. "Power and respect," He repeatedly mocked whilst studying the board for his next move in the game. Sensi shifted in his seat uncomfortably whilst Essen laughed his old school theories off, but deep down he knew Essen would heed his words. He had known Essen since the late 70s. Back when Essen was a little ashy kneed boy, now sitting before him a man. A worthy opponent if he had to choose one. Essen had long showed his loyalty and devotion to the detective, unlike his own son Judas. The two men were the complete opposite, yet they would die for each other if they were given the chance. Essen was humble, well-educated and level headed whilst Judas's arrogance and attractive looks prevailed over all other abilities in his line of work. Judas was ineffective when it came to following direct orders; therefore making any type of decisions on his own regarding the team was forbidden. Sensi had to resort to manipulation to get his 34-year-old son to adhere to the significant role the detective had fought so hard for him to obtain. "Fuck all that Mr. M! I got your power and respect right here!" said Essen seriously, as he lifted up the bottom of his t-shirt for the detective to glance at the 9 mm handgun tucked between his jeans, and pressed up securely against his waist. "And you don't ever have to worry about your people smelling me either." He brushed his hand against the steel, covering it back up before turning his attention back to the table as Sensi made his move. People in Hackney sang Essen's praises like Brooklyn did Jay-Z's, except Essen was much darker in complexion and of Nigerian decent. At age 35, Essen owned properties in Lagos, Nigeria, a town house in LA and a £259,000 penthouse apartment in London where he currently laid his head. Essen was always neat and clean shaven, and dressed from head to toe in black. Yet, he never drowned himself in the latest designer clothes or jewels as Judas did. However, whether 'all blingged out' or not, the females in the hood stayed on his dick 24/7. While Essen wasn't as flashy with his things, he still had swag; it's just his priorities laid elsewhere. As the young victim of a village fire that stole his parents' and younger brother, Essen had come to England as a child, craving the love and compassion that was stolen from him when his family died. He stayed true to his roots and educated himself on his Nigerian heritage and culture, proudly wearing it on his sleeve. No woman had ever come close to replacing the love that he'd once had as a child, or filling the void that had long taken residence in his heart. "Now we're playing chess." Essen said rubbing his hands together over the board. He sat up straight in his seat, and a rush of excitement rushed through him as he watched the detective take out the same bishop who had taken out his pawn. "You should be careful who you send out to do your bidding Essen. Was it worth risking an important player so early in the game?" Sensi asked. He saw that he had his opponent's queen covered, and attempted to call his bluff. "Well ain't this a bitch." Essen muttered whilst his eyes darted over the board. "You got me backed up yeah, I'll admit that, but I ain't ready to pack it up yet. You got me seriously twisted if you think I'm about to cry over a fuckin bishop when I got so many players left in the game." Essen screwed up his face in concentration. "In about two minutes, I'm gonna steel your knight who you've been neglecting, leaving you with no option but to protect your own damn bitch. And before you can even think of a plan to attack, my baby will have moved and I'll be one step closer to tapping your girl's ass." Essen said doubled over in laughter.

"But you lost three." Sensi said sternly, no longer concerned with the playing pieces on the board. "What you talking about?" Essen composed himself meeting eyes with the detective, forgetting about the game. "You lost three men today damnit," Sensi growled pounding the playing table with his fist causing the pieces to topple over and out of place on the board. 'I knew this nigga had something up his ass,' Essen thought, as he looked up calmly at the Detective. "Again we find ourselves in an uncomfortable place, a place where we both have to step out of our comfort zones to put right what the people around us have done wrong. I know I've already asked much of you Essen but this is something I cannot administrate on my own." The detective said as he stood up, removing himself from the game. "Walk with me to my car." Sensi commanded over his shoulder, slowly walking to the entrance of the park where he had parked his car by the pavement on the side of the road. Essen slowly removed himself from the playing table and caught up with him, and together they both walked through the dimly lit park in silence until they had reached their parked cars. "Your bishops can't be trusted," the detective said firmly, unlocking his car door. "I already have a confession of breaking an entry along with an attempted robbery on tape from two of your guys, and the others can only remain silent for so long." "Where did you find these little cunts?" the detective demanded, looking back at Essen. "You're asking the wrong man." Essen held up his hands, "You know I don't fuck with outsiders. Judas does the recruiting when it comes to the team, and I've been laying low after that shit you put me down on a couple of months back. All I know is there're a couple of knuckle-heads from down south trying to put in some work to make a little dough." "Best thing for you to do is to send 'em home with a warning or drop 'em a little thinking time." He suggested, hoping the old man would show some heart and spare the kid's hard time. "Nah, it's just too big of a risk Essen, the Superintendent can't find out about this operation. I won't let some south slanging hoodlums ruin my reputation; not now that I've brought us this far," Sensi responded raising his voice as he got into his black, tinted M3 BMW, and buckled up. "I said I got you Mr. M." Essen stressed patting his tool through his shirt. He leaned back on the park railings and tried to convince the Detective to calm down. "They're just a bunch of kids, they don't have anything on me or Judas, and they sure as hell haven't got shit on you," he calmly said. "No, we need to deal with this and see it through." Sensi said almost paranoid as he revved up the engine. He shut his door and rolled down the window. "I really appreciate what you did for me Essen. I know I don't need to ask if you read what was in that file you tracked down for me." "Say no more Mr. M". Essen replied understanding his old friend well. Three months ago the Detective had him track down a private investigator that had been employed to do some digging. He'd pulled up some files dirty enough to not only denounce the Detective's name and end his career, but also land him in jail. Sensi had a fair amount of skeletons in his closet but it was nothing that Essen could judge him on. "Same time next week yeah?" Essen suggested, referring to his and the Detective's weekly chess game in the park. "Of course Essen, I'll be in touch, but I don't wanna smell you until then." Sensi laughed as he pulled another cigar out his inside pocket and balanced it in his mouth before putting his foot down and speeding off into the darkness of the night.

Chapter 2

"Is there something I can assist you ladies with?" asked a young, pale skinned store clerk who stood posted at the front desk. She cleared her throat in order to attract the attention of the three ladies who had entered the elegant boutique in Hampstead Heath. The ladies paid the clerk, along with a middle aged white couple who seemed to be having some kind of relationship break down in the far end of the store, little to no-mind. Instead, they greeted the small, stocky, security guard who stood at the entrance with a smile, then separated throughout the store slipping cautiously into their positions. "Umm, Ladies, can I help you?" asked the store clerk once again, whose name tag read 'Ginger.' She approached them all, but was clearly speaking to Brittany. "No, no thank you. Not right now." Brittany politely responded stunning the girl with her smile. Her olive tanned completion and jet black hair always gave her a lot of attention, but not even her blue eyes could out shine the gold-plated tooth she'd had set in when she was seventeen. Slightly intimidated the store clerk backed off but kept her eyes glued on the breathtaking image of the woman before her. Every Saturday for the past eight months, Ginger assisted Brittany while she visited Pandora, just watching as she did her thing. The store clerks in Hampstead Heath paid little attention to their wealthy customers and had proved to be exceptionally trusting when it came to their clients paying for their purchases by cheque. The last time Brittany had visited Pandora, she'd travelled alone and written more than £18,000 in counterfeit cheques. Today she planned on doubling that amount, because after tonight she would be abandoning her grind forever. In the last few weeks, Brittany had hit Lakeside, Birmingham Mall and the West End writing no less than forty dud cheques. The items that she picked up today, minus what she kept for herself, could sell for at least £37,000 on the streets. Her boyfriend Craig's sister, Jessica, who worked in a bank, re-printed customers' cheque books for 40% of Brittany's earnings. Her girlfriend Shelly usually sold most of the women's clothing and accessories to the girls at Sainsburys where she worked. Her customers would snoop around the stores, and then tell Shelly what they wanted. No one could say Brittany's prices weren't negotiable or affordable, but with Craig disappearing off the face of the earth and his sister Jessica not returning any of her calls, Brittany was being forced to put down her pen and retire. Brittany was what she liked to be called, 'Caucasian tanned,' with jet-black hair and a traditional pointy Jewish nose, but her body was shaped like an Afro-Caribbean's. With an all-natural pair of double D's that sat high upon her chest, thick thighs and rounded hips, she had earned the nick name 'Big Booty Britt.' Growing up, her mother had put her weight gain down to the amount of time Brittany spent eating at the Henderson's house next door. "Jerk chicken, green bananas, fried yams, rice and peas are not a normal part of a white girl's diet." Her mother would often mutter this under her breath when Brittany and Sydney would jump the garden fence, climbing from one house to another, getting permission from their parents to spent time at one another's homes after school. "You know those aren't going to fit you right?" said Sydney with raised eyebrows, her hands half tucked in the back pockets of her jeans. She strode over to where Brittany stood with various items of clothing slung over her arm and commented on a pair of jeans Brittany had taken off the sales rack and thrown into her basket. "I know that." Brittany exclaimed. "Most of this shit isn't for me. These jeans are for a customer in Camden. She's a little heavier than me but her waist is kinda small," she whispered putting her basket down and sizing up a pair of custom dark blue denim jeans made by Victoria Beckham next to the ones she wore. "You want me to see if they got 'em in your size?" Brittany said already rummaging through the rack. "I'm telling you Syd, these VB Jeans are what's up right now. And at £468 a pair, it doesn't matter if they fit. A fat bitch could squeeze into a size 10 and have a River Island wearing bitch looking a mess." Sydney glanced at the item and nodded with no reply. She watched as Brittany turned around and continued her weekend ritual of checking labels and sizes before pulling expensive items that neither of them could afford off the shelves, and tossing them in her basket. She knew Brittany's temperament with her over the past few days had been short; Sydney's constant sneaking around and lying generally went unnoticed, but lately it was quite the opposite. Her frame of mind had been unsettled by a disturbing call. 'Maybe it's those fucking green pills, got me hearing all kinds of shit, fucking with my mind,' Sydney thought, as she caught a glimpse of herself in the stores full-length mirror and examined her reflection from afar. She was blessed with features that Brittany couldn't compete with. Sydney's cool chocolate skin complexion was flawless, put together with the dimples indented in her cheeks and her head full of silky, bouncy shoulder-length curls. Plus, add in her thick hips and curves, and there hadn't been a man as far as Sydney could remember that had passed her on the streets without doing a double take. Sydney used to have that 'I can turn a gay man straight before the bitch turns me down' sexiness about her. Though that had been two years ago, it had been a long time since she'd been on the road with her girls, and even longer since she'd been herself. "Thank you for shopping at Pandora Mrs. Havagan, please come again," said the new girl posted at the front desk, shaking Brittany's hand excitedly before she handed her four customized Pandora shopping bags and a receipt. "No, thank you Danni." Brittany said reading the petite girl's name tag. The new store clerk who had come out from the back, and was now posted at the front desk replacing the Ginger who had been so engrossed in the figures she punched in the calculator that she hadn't seen Brittany snatch a stone coloured designer purse from the counter opposite them, nor had she paid attention to the dud cheque Brittany had written out of a near empty cheque book and placed boldly in her hand. Sydney couldn't help but let out short sounds of distress in the small confined space of the elevator. She shifted endlessly where she stood, and repositioned herself twice before the elevator doors opened onto Hampstead Heath's Shopping Centre's ground floor car park. "You know what Syd, I'm done. When we get back to the End's, I'm dropping your ass off at a bus stop unless we pass a cab station on the way outta here. This is stupid and you know it, but if you wanna keep playing this game then fine." Brittany said escaping the crowded elevator crippled with bags. She walked ahead of the two girls in a miserable huff, sucking her teeth loudly for passersby to hear while hurrying herself through the crowd until she was out of Sydney and Shelly's sights. "Damn Syd, what's up with that?" said a shocked Shelly as she turned to Sydney. "Britt!" Shelley called after Brittany, though not loud enough for her to hear. "What the hell's going on between the two of you?" Shelly stopped to ask Sydney again, seeing as her question had gone heard and unanswered the first time she'd asked. Shelly wasn't feisty and loud like Sydney and Brittany, but she knew how to get her claws out and pounce when she found herself surrounded with her back against the wall. Just standing over 5ft with a curvaceous but, stocky frame, Shelly was considered cute-enough. She was reliant on Brittany and Sydney's presence in her life; they were all she had. Sydney's own mother had deliver Special, Shelly's daughter, when she found herself in labor at just thirteen. Shelly looked at Sydney who showed no signs of backing down and decided it was time for her to step in now.

"Should I just assume you're behind all this animosity or are you gonna give it to me straight?" Shelly asked Sydney anticipating her reply. "Brittany saw us last night, we got into it, and now we're just ignoring each other apart from the small talk." Sydney said and sighed, unable to look Shelly directly in the eye. "She knows about you and Judas?" Shelly asked shocked, almost not believing what she'd just heard. "Yeah she knows about me and Judas, I just said she saw us last night didn't I?" Sydney snapped. "Calm down Sydney!" Shelly retorted, feeding Sydney the same attitude she'd fed her. "So, she saw you and Judas together, you know Britt, she ain't gonna remember shit after a few drinks, and it's not like she's gonna go around spreading the word. Who's she gonna tell?" "Brittany's your best friend." Shelly continued whilst she and Sydney began to slowly make their way through the bulk of commuting shoppers towards Brittany's car. "Shelly, don't patronize me. Brittany plays like she's innocent but you know what she's really like. Brittany picks her friends when she needs 'em, and I mean that shit for real. I gave her a bed last night, and when I asked her what the deal was with her not going home, she point blank told me to mind my own business, so when she caught me and Judas hugged up, I dropped the same line and told her to stay outta mines. Fuck knows, why she's trying to be all up in my business now, when she didn't give a damn when I was locked up in Tailsdale or Cleverfield," Sydney replied unfazed. "That's fucked up Syd, you ain't being fair. Brittany dragged her ass to every clinic you were admitted to, she even helped you to escape a number of times, we both did. Brittany ain't the same person she used to be before you were admitted to Cleverfield, you know. Neither of us are, and it's fucked up too, because Brittany's really missed you Syd. Ever since she broke up with Craig..." Shelly began to explain but was interrupted by Sydney's gasp. "Wait," Sydney cut her off before she could say anymore. "Candy Craig!" She giggled like a little girl. "Yeah Candy Craig, but nobody around the way calls him that anymore. It's Cee, and nigga's can't fuck with him like that," Shelly said educating Sydney on the changes in their hood. "Britt and Cee's been together officially for over a year now," Shelley continued. "At first they were just fucking, you know how she does, but then they seemed to be settling down. Britt was feeling Cee differently and Cee must have felt the same because he doesn't let any girls stay where he lays his head, and before he got with Britt I heard he didn't even fuck at his place. Yet, a few months back Cee moved Britt in." Sydney looked at Shelly disbelieving. 'Brittany settling down, yeah right,' she thought. "I'm telling you Syd, they were vibing on a different level. Britt and Craig we're stacking mad paper until some fools from the South or wherever hit him up for his product last week. I took Brittany to the hospital that night, and she's lucky too, because the word on the block is that Cee barely made it out of his flat with his life." "The Hospital," Sydney shrieked, more concerned with Brittany than with Craig. Brittany hardly ever got sick. "She had an abortion Syd, but she didn't want Craig to know. She spent the night in Whipps Cross Hospital because she didn't wanna be spotted at Homerton by anyone in the hood," Shelley whispered. "So what happened to

Craig?" Sydney asked not knowing what to say about Brittany and her decision to terminate her child. "Like I said, I was at the Hospital with Britt, so I don't know. But I do know that Brittany hasn't heard or seen Craig since, and the word on the street is that Brittany called the hit." Again, Shelly lowered her voice as they approached Brittany's car. Sydney opened the door and sat in the passenger's seat despite the tension between Brittany and herself whilst Shelly sat comfortably in the back. "So what's the deal with Craig, I mean Cee?" Sydney turned and whispered to Shelly after Brittany slammed shut the boot. "Do you think Brittany set him up, and pulled this whole abortion stunt to use as an alibi?" she asked while Brittany stood fixing her hair using the reflection of her cars tinted glass. "What? Syd that's sick!" replied Shelly, snapping her neck around to look at Sydney like she was crazy. "I said Cee and Britt were stacking together. Besides, we drove by their flat the following afternoon, and their neighbors said Cee was packed up and gone before the police arrived." "They saw him jump over the fence and run through the back gate while the perpetrators' were straight up busted trying to unscrew Cee's plasma off the wall." Shelly continued as she rested her head on the headrest while Sydney listened, all the while shaking her head. "Brittany just wouldn't do something like that; she's been fucked up about that shit since it went down." "Damn, I don't blame her." Sydney finally said. "I can't even imagine Craig on his grind, let alone Brittany fucking with him and them both getting it in." "You're telling me the truth right, Craig and Brittany?" Sydney quietly laughed to herself, and then turned her attention to her window as Brittany seemed to be having some kind of bitter discussion with the security guard they'd greeted outside Pandora. "Ah wah ya ave fa mi Brit-Annie?" said the West Indian sounding security guard, as he licked his lips smiling and showing a grill full of rotten teeth. He used a soiled, white cloth to wipe the sweat dripping from his brow, before placing it in his back pocket where he'd taken it from. The Bernie Mac looking man wheezed heavily, looked Brittany up and down, and then stuck his hand out waiting for Brittany to put in his palm the only thing his heart desired, and their reason for visiting Hampstead Heath's Shopping Centre this afternoon. "Freddie put your fucking hand down." Brittany snapped, shaking her head in disbelief. She surveyed the parking lot discreetly to make sure no one was eyeing her before reaching into her purse and retrieving the small rock of cocaine the crack addict security guard had been pestering her for all day. She held the last of her stash in the palm of her hand. "Fred, there's a situation up here that needs your attention." A voice called from the guard's walkie-talkie. Quickly, Freddie grabbed the rock out of Brittany's hand and shoved it deep into his front pocket before detaching his walkie- talkie from his waist band and turning to leave. "Excuse me!" Brittany shrieked, with her hand held out, "My money you fat fuck!" she called after him. "Put your fucking hand down," Freddie laughed making his way through the crowd before Brittany could get another word in. He muttered something about a warning and it going before destruction, but it was something Brittany didn't care to hear as she composed herself and got into her car determined to put Freddie, and her crack selling days behind her. "What the hell Brittany!" shouted Shelly in protest, at the way Brittany had slammed her car door shut, thrown herself in the driver's seat and frantically pushed the key in the ignition of her cherry red Audi A3, then stuck her head out the window as she backed out of her space. "Move out the fucking way or imma back the fuck into your car!" She yelled out, banging on the steering wheel at the fools who thought they'd have a better chance of getting into her space if they waited up her ass. Brittany revved her engine to let the people behind her know she was reversing, and that she had no problem fucking up their ride. She looked up into her rear-view mirror, and cursed when she noticed the ginger-headed clerk from Pandora standing on the second floor pointing her car out to a set of security guards heading their way. Freddie was hot on her heels too. "Syd look in your mirror, and tell me that I'm not paranoid?" Brittany asked, wanting to get her opinion. "You're not paranoid Britt, their on to us." Sydney reported back, and sunk down in her seat. She began to panic seeing the guards making their way down the escalators, heading towards them. It almost reminded her of those nights in Cleverfield when she'd attempted to escape. She closed her eyes in an attempt to drown out the noise. "Back the fuck up!" Brittany frantically screamed out of her window to a 'Good Samaritan' who had attempted to block them in. The bald headed man did as he was told just seconds before one of the guards grabbed, and tried to pull open the passenger side door. "I suggest you stop this right now before this gets worse than it needs to be," a heavy built security guard commanded, but Brittany wasn't having any of it. She backed out of her parking space and headed towards the nearest exit, hitting the highway at full speed.

Chapter 3

"WHAT?" yelled Judas into the mouthpiece of his apartment's cordless phone. He was still half asleep when the private caller had rung, stopped, and then rung again, determined to wake him up. "It's nice to hear from you too Judas. Did I catch you at a bad time?" spat Stitches, the mother of his youngest-child, with venom at him through the phone. Judas sighed, rubbing the sleep from his eyes as he looked towards his nightstand, reading the time on the digital clock that sat beside a picture of him and his fiancée Naomi on their recent vacation to the South of France. "You need to stop doing this Stitches," spoke Judas calmly into the phone. Stitches had recently started playing mind games with him and Naomi by calling and hanging up on their home phone in an attempt to wind Naomi up, which usually had Judas fired up and banging on her door. "Stop what Judas? Stop feeding your daughter? Tameerah hasn't seen you in a week. What do you think she eats, fresh fucking air?" Stitches rhetorically asked, and Judas could have sworn he felt her smile through the phone. Judas had first met Stitches when he rushed his man Sticks to

Homerton Hospital after he'd been stabbed and was admitted into ICU. Back then Stitches was a student-nurse, and was training in Homerton Hospital in the emergency ward, stitching up and tending to patients minor wounds. Judas had been cut during the brawl, but had refused to be treated; he had to be on point for Sticks. He didn't have time to play 21 questions with the doctors or the police. Stitches had come across as a gullible, but well educated university student, innocent to the world, though she lived and worked in the heart of the hood. Her 'no questions asked' mentality was what had drawn Judas to her from the jump. Stitches had taken Judas home that very night, stitched him up, and then giggled like a schoolgirl when he gave her the nickname 'Stitches' after gratefully admiring her work. She was Nurse Reid by day and Stitches by night. It wasn't long before Stitches was upgraded from Judas's bed to a permanent position on his payroll. Now she stitched up and cleaned the wounds of various criminals who were wealthy enough to pay Judas for her trade. Her clients entered her ground floor flat through the back door into her kitchen, and after she got to work on them, Judas would go to work on her. At twenty-two Stitches had a figure that should have been oiled down and showcased in a magazine. It was almost impossible for Judas to resist hitting it from behind at least once, after watching her bend over to attend to his bleeding wound. Stitches was a car crash in the bedroom and her head game was D.O.A. She worked her ass off for Judas, but her unexpected pregnancy took the fun out of whatever it was she assumed they had. "What can I do for you Stitches?"

Judas asked in his 'Don't fuck with me' tone. "I miss you Judas, we both miss you. It's not even about the money." Stitches admitted. Judas had promised Stitches a lifetime together, their seven-year-old daughter was approaching eight and had yet to see even 24 hours with the man she called dad. "Look Stitches, you need to stop pushing this bullshit idea of us being together," Judas said reaching out for the framed photo on the nightstand beside his bed. Stitches had been getting on Naomi's last nerve with her games, and she was starting to get on Judas's nerves too. "Why do we have to put a label on what we got and call it a family?" Judas asked. He loved the sexual energy he had with Stitches, but hated the hold she had on him when it came to their child. Judas held on to the picture frame and looked into the face of his first love. "Because we are a family Judas, we don't have a choice in this matter. You are Tameerah's father, and she's your child, unfortunately, she deserves your love." Stitches pronounced in her defense. "Well I can't do it." Judas said point blankly, and placed the photo on the bed. He sat up straight, and yawned aloud. "I make sure you and my daughter are nice don't I? What more do you want?" "Sending strange men to our house at all hours of the night is not making sure we're nice!" Stitches said in frustration and sniffed. "What happened to keeping us safe, you just giving out my address now? Nigga's pay for their treatment and you tell them where?" She sobbed. "Stitches you know I can't be up and down in these streets, I ain't got time to be running people by your house when their hot. I ain't going to jail for some bullshit neither," Judas explained with a sly smile of his own.

"Bullshit!" shouted Stitches. "Come on girl, you know what I mean. Swishing your ass around in your shorts around them dope boys that roll through after a throw down," Judas smirked. He knew Stitches would be racking her brain trying to find out how he knew about that incident seeing as they were classified customers of her own. "It's all good Stitches, you do you." Judas chuckled. "Get that money how you need to get it during the week, and I'll see you at my mother's house on Sunday afternoon." "You know what, fuck you Judas," Stitches sulked, "Your mother's house is like a sauna and your other baby momma's get on my damn nerves, especially that Keion." "Hello!" She shouted after realizing Judas hadn't responded in a while. "Are you even listening to me?" "Yeah I'm listening to you Stitches, I just don't care. I'm about fed up with all this Sunday lunch crap as much as you women are, but Tameerah, Shayanne, Brooklyn, Ameerah and Kayla are sisters, so get over it!" Judas spat. "There ain't shit I can do about the situation but deal with it." Stitches disconnected the call. "Stupid bitch," Judas muttered, and then sat silent hearing that the line was still open and hadn't gone dead. "Hello, Judas," a voice of authority said through the open line. "Who's dat...?" Judas cautiously asked. "It's your father you ugly shit, but you would have known that if you hadn't had me waiting on the other line for so god-damned long." Judas heard his father bellow into the phone. "Dad, what's up? I didn't even hear the other line beep." "Look... I know what you're gonna say, but just let me explain?" Judas sat up straight and adjusted his position on the bed. He and his father ran a lucrative theft and laundering operation within the Metropolitan Law enforcement. Since joining the Force, his father, Sensi Mendez had been involved in 27 raids since November of '99. One of which resulted in the murder of Gerald Hastings, and another in connection to the fall of the Henderson's reign. Sensi was one of four officers assigned to the Henderson Case. After ginning up a story to obtain a search warrant to the Henderson's home address, Sensi had his team do a no-knock entry, which resulted in an officer shooting and wounding the leader. The officers then planted heroin in their basement and asked another informant to lie on the enforcement's behalf in an attempt to cover up their intentions. Two officers pled guilty to county charges of voluntary manslaughter and a charge of violating constitutional rights. They were currently sitting in county prisons, both serving 7 year sentences. Detective Greenham, the only one to go to trial, had been prosecuted and charged with the lesser crime of making a false statement to an investigator and violating his oath of office. Greenham faced up to 16 years in prison if convicted, leaving his position wide open for the taking. Sensi was highly praised by his team, who were oblivious to the fact he was a street informant. He'd instantly seized the opportunity presented before him, and soon enough was promoted to Major on his own technicalities. A male protagonist by all accounts, Detective Mendez had the district eating out of his hands. When he'd cunningly informed the law enforcement community about the Henderson's profitable drug activity, whilst manipulating other officers to step out of their line of duty, he'd masterfully dictated both sides. The Henderson's were ruthless in their dealings and Sensi despised the fact that they had members of law enforcement on their payroll, something that just wasn't going to happen on his watch. When the dust had settled, and the transfer was made, the Superintendent of London was singing Sensi's praises for his work on the investigation and helping to bring down Hackney's most notorious drug lords. Detective Greenham's participation in the conspiracy had law enforcement using him as a prime example to any other officer thinking about manipulating the system. The Superintendent made plans to have him publicly humiliated then sent to prison to rot, but Greenham had other ideas. Determined not to go down without a fight, Greenham sought the expertise of a private investigator, and dug up an incriminating past during an enhanced background check against Sensi and the other three officers involved in the corruption case. Unfortunately for him, his investigator was killed in a fatal road crash whilst on his way to report his findings. Greenham was sentenced to 13 years in prison under the constitutional rights law, where he only lasted six months. Sensi had known it wouldn't be long before Greenham's body would be found hanging from the light cord in his cell, and he was right. Sensi parked his car crookedly beside a parking inspector, rolled down his window, and opened his glove compartment to retrieve a cigar he had lusted after since breakfast this morning. His current piece of ass was asthmatic, and would be coughing and spitting at even the slightest hint of smoke. "I'm listening," he said. He rolled his eyes while leaning back in his seat and preceded to light his cigar with the car's built in lighter. It was predictable for Judas to let his temperament get the better of him, ending all possible logical thought, and causing him to fail where instructions were concerned. "I fucked up dad, I know. But in my defense I didn't know that was your raid, I didn't even know you had any of my guys under investigation," Judas said doubting his father even knew how he operated on the streets. "Craig's been walking around with his pockets full for some time now, and I figured it was time I reminded him who was boss," he explained agitated. "By sending three incompetent rough-necks to rob him before a federal raid," replied sarcastically while Sensi coughing and shifting in his seat. He sat parked two buildings down from the local picture house awaiting the beginning of his show. "Is it not enough that you're the sole distributor of this district? Are you not content with the status you hold?" Sensi asked. "Your stupidity landed three files on my desk and a whole bunch of questions that I have to make go away. Honestly Judas, it is imperative that you have these dealers in your debt. You're constantly competing in your own competitions, setting the bar just high enough for you to reach and for everybody else to touch. Judas, one day you'll realize that power is not strength but numbers. Now is not the time for a war, not whilst were living good." Sensi advised remembering how little power he'd held during the Henderson's reign. Sensi knew more about the streets than he cared for his son to know. He also knew first hand that it was better to be the power behind the scenes, than to be the icon of your trade.

Chapter 4

Essen casually strode towards a hefty ticket attendant in Rio's picture-house dressed in a rugged pair of black Levis, a simple black t-shirt covered by a baseball jacket, and a crisp black pair of Air Force Ones on his feet. He handed the woman his ticket, and waited to be shown to his screen. "Thank you Sir, its screen four right ahead," the cheerful woman instructed, taking his ticket and letting him through the double screen doors. He held a large bag of popcorn under his arm, a large plastic disposable cup of Coke in one hand, and with his free hand, he held the screen door open for a group of teenage girls who giggled when they bounced past him popping their gum. Essen entered the screen with ease, and seeing that the film's adverts had started and most of the seats were full except for a few at the back, vigilantly slipped into the shadows, and snuck into a side chair close to the screens exit next to a brother who clapped his hands, obviously hyped by the trailer of a film. Forty minutes into the film and the ambiance in the room was tense. The sounds of guns blazing while actor Denzel Washington fought a feud in his latest film, 'American

Gangster' had the audience in awe. Essen seized his opportunity to shuffle down in his chair and drop two seats below, stopping beside his mark in the dark. He moved into the shadows where he couldn't be seen and screwed the silencer onto his 6 inch Colt Python Revolver, which he had kept hidden in his popcorn bag until now. The Python was his old friend. He stood inches away from his victim, watching as the actors continued to eliminate their opponents before he fired a single shot, catching his victim dead in the throat. The man's head fell to the side, and he caught a glimpse of his killer before gurgling and grunting on his own blood, and struggling to take his last breath. Essen looked up at the screen again to see the bloodshed and mayhem was over, much like the life of his victim. "Their dropping like flies man," the two hundred pound brother beside Essen chuckled; he had slipped back into his seat unnoticed, and was sitting sipping at his coke through a straw. Both men shared a few friendly words then continued to watch the film until the credits rolled up and the lights came on. "Nah, that film was serious," the man said, turning to Essen before getting up to leave, only to find that he'd already slipped out. "Wankster," he chuckled to himself as he was being escorted out of the building by one of the many police officers strangely filling up the screen. Essen watched from car parked across the street as the police rounded up the majority of screen four for questioning before turning his attention to the young girl who trembled uncontrollably in another officer's arms. The teenager had spent the last half hour next to her father's lifeless body, and was now covered in seventy percent of his blood from her struggle with the paramedics when she'd begged them to revive him, though he was pronounced dead at the scene. Essen had turned his attention away from the scene for a second, when the real action started. "DROP YOUR BAG NOW!" An armed, uniformed, officer shouted ready to fire on command. The two hundred pound brother held his hands up high above his head, and immediately dropped the contents he held, causing the gun that Essen had placed with him to fire, flattening the tire of a marked police vehicle. "I ain't done anything man; I swear, I ain't ever seen that thing before," he roared as he was restrained to the ground. People looked on as armed officers surrounded him with their weapons drawn, praying they'd get the chance to dissemble his body in the streets. "You enjoying the show boy?" Sensi crept up and asked with sarcasm, snapping Essen out of his thoughts. Sensi stood at 6ft, and was broad shouldered much like his son. Sensi and Judas were so much alike, that the only thing to define the two was age. Judas had that 'good-hair' women prayed their children would inherit as did Sensi, and they both shared the same dashing smile casing a row of perfect white teeth. A whole generation before signing up for his badge, Sensi was known as the right-hand man of one of the most respected men in East London, Andy Henderson AKA Lock-Ness. Lock-Ness and Sensi went way back, as far as their late teens. Sensi was the mind and muscle behind Lock's hood fame, and in his opinion, all Lock had was charm. Still, they were boys, and together they started a lucrative drug operation, posing as respectable businessmen while trafficking heroin and cocaine through the district of the East End. But after years of violence and bloodshed, Lock-Ness claimed the top spot in town, cementing his legend in the hood. No amount of food moved in or out of East London without Sensi or Lock's OK. However, Sensi had other plans. He grew tired of being passed off as some old has-been bodyguard. Exchanging his player's card for a shiny badge made him the real boss in his hometown, but his actions caused havoc all around Hackney. And when word got back to Lock-Ness that his boy was working for the feds, his comrades on the streets grew angry with betrayal. Sensi had won over a small part of the town and had lived lavishly until he'd eaten up his stash and was left with two options, live cheque to cheque, or crawl back to his ex-partner in crime. At the time, Sensi had cringed at the idea of groveling to Lock. But what was a little animosity between friends? Sensi approached Lock with a humble heart; he explained that it would be beneficial for them to do business together again and, how convenient it was to have friends in high places. "For you brother, I can get you first-hand information on raids, investigations, provide you with federal weapons and even…" Armor, was what Sensi was about to say, before Lock spat in his face. He damn near ripped off his badge in disgust, raving to his surrounding crew, who already had their hands on their machines in case Sensi felt brave, that Sensi had completely sold out, and the only reprieve Lock had promised him for his betrayal was a slow death. "There are no friends in the feds, just snitches." Lock had spat. Today, Sensi could hold his head up high and smile. 'Had he taken up my offer that armor would have come in handy.' He chuckled his way into a cough. "You alright Mr. M?" Essen asked, unlocking the passenger door for the detective to take a seat. Together they sat in silence watching the scene before them unfold. "Congratulations." Sensi finally said, not once taking his eyes off the scene. "I didn't wanna say anything before because I thought it might throw you off your game, but the man you just assassinated was Jeffrey Perkins." The Detective coughed again before retrieving his inhaler from his pocket. 'Jeffrey Perkins,' Essen thought, knowing he'd heard the name before, but couldn't quite place the acquaintance. Essen thought hard. "I'm not following," he replied confused. He watched the detective place his inhaler between his lips and struggle for air, before placing it securely back in his pocket to put in its place a cigar. Essen turned his attention back to the scene, making eye contact with the fifteen-year-old daughter of the deceased. He now had a recollection of Jeffrey Perkins. He knew exactly who he had been ordered to kill.

PENAL CODE
Section 487(d)(1)
GRAND THEFT AUTO

Billie Dureyea Shell

Chapter 1

THE SPOKESMAN

The Spokesman woke up on this beautiful morning not feeling any sympathy or the slightest regret for what he's about to handle. The work must be done. The only thing he had swimming in his mind. The work must be done. No matter the consequences. He got up from his king size bed and stretched. He walked over to the window and opened the curtains. What a wonderful day it is, he thought. Finally, I will get what's mine. He took a quick shower and sang love songs the entire time. He got out of the shower and continued to give himself the nicest shaven face you will ever see. Got to look good for the big day. He went into his closet and picked out his street gear. He put on a tee-shirt, jeans, Air Force 1's and an Atlanta fitted cap. He took one look in the mirror. Damn, I look good. He shut the closet door before going into the kitchen. He made himself a nice peanut butter and jelly sandwich. He sat at the dining room table and flipped through his contact list while he ate. "Here we go." He muttered with a mouth full. He removed a card and stared at it to make sure it was the correct one. Absolutely, it was the one. He read the words across the card to himself. "Private Investigator, Lenny Daverson." He hated Lenny with every ounce of blood he possessed in his body. But today, today he needed him. Today was the day he would love him. Today, if he paid close attention and did his job the way detectives are supposed to. Lenny would make him the happiest man in the entire world. He took the final bite of his sandwich and flipped the card into his pocket. No more delays, he must act now before he would miss this perfect opportunity. The work must be done. He grabbed his car keys and headed for the door. He locked up the house and got into his car. He sang along with Usher while he drove to the other side of town. Out of sight, out of mind. He thought about this situation numerous times before. This was definitely the best way to handle it. He found a busy gas station. Good mixed crowd. Nobody on this side of town would notice him. He parked his car at pump eight. He went inside and paid for some gas. He walked pass his vehicle without bothering to set the system up. He thought if someone was to notice him. They would approach him while he's standing at the car pumping gas or on the pay phone. His mind decided to handle that instantly. The pay phone was at the far end of the gas station. He walked over nonchalant, not wanting anybody to notice him. He retrieved the card from his pocket. He lifted the phone and dialed the private investigator's number. The phone rang three times and a woman answered. "Hold please." One minute later detective Lenny answered. "This is Inspector Daverson." The Spokesman smiled. "Let's get to the point. You're looking for Twenty, right?" Lenny felt his spine quiver. "Who is this?" "Does it matter? All you need to understand is that I know the time and place Twenty's next lift will be. Get your pen and pad."

Chapter 2

BLIND MAN

Twenty stepped out onto his room balcony. "Damn it feels good outside." Today is payday for him. Later tonight, he is going to lift the last car on the list for a buyer name, Money. The car is a 1969 Boss 302. Money, a notorious drug dealer on the other side of town who loves old school cars. He created a list of his fifteen most wanted cars and hired the best car thief around to handle the job. Each car was valued over $100,000. The job is for one million dollars and the man who is known to be the best, is Twenty. He has been lifting vehicles for anybody who had money since he was seventeen. This is the way he survives. He even has his own crew called, The Lifters. Three years of lifting vehicles professionally and this one is going to be his biggest payout. He has already received half the money up front and the other half he would get when the job is completed. His team of lifters included his best friend,

Jeff. He has known Jeff since the first grade. The second member of his team is Paula. They met Paula when they were thirteen years old. They lifted their first car in a grocery store parking lot. They saw a 96' Chevy Impala on 26-inch rims left running. They thought the car was beautiful and Twenty wanted it. It's funny how your best friend gets dragged into tough situations. Although, Jeff wasn't about to let Twenty steal the car all by himself. The coast was clear. At least, they thought the coast was clear. Twenty rushed over to the vehicle with Jeff close behind. Twenty hopped in the driver seat and Jeff hopped in the passenger's. Twenty put the car in drive and floored the pedal burning out of the parking lot. They got halfway down the block before hearing a voice in the back seat. It was Paula waking up from her nap. "What are you doing in my dad's car?" She asked sheepishly. Twenty was super excited about lifting his first car that he didn't notice the girl in the back seat. "What the hell!" He swerved the car because he was a little nervous that there was someone in the car with them. "A girl is in the back seat!" Jeff yelled hysterically. "What's going on?" Paula climbed over the front seat. "What are you doing little girl?" Twenty asked. He swerved the car back on track. "I'm twelve going on thirteen. In one month I'll be a teenager for your information. I'm not little." Paula answered with attitude.

"Twenty!" Jeff yelled. "We got to get out of this car for the police come. I don't want to go to jail man. I'm only thirteen." "Shut up you big baby." Paula hissed without knowing what was going on. "Why would the police come?" Twenty turned to her attention. Suddenly, he was struck by her beauty. This was the prettiest girl he has ever seen in his life. She had caramel skin, brown hair, and hazel eyes. He was lost for words while staring at her. How was he to answer? "Twenty!" Jeff yelled hysterically. Twenty focused back on the road. He had swerved into oncoming traffic. "Shit!" A car was coming right at them. He maneuvered the Chevy back into the proper lane. The Impala kept swerving out of control and they hit a fire hydrant. The boys got out and ran for it. Jeff took off first and Twenty was right behind him, but he stopped. He ran back to the car. "Hey… hey! You ok!" Paula didn't move. He pulled her from the car. She hit her head pretty good on the dashboard. Too late to run. The police showed. They took Twenty away and he got put on probation until he was eighteen. Paula would never forget what he did by coming back for her. The next time they had met was their tenth-grade year. Ever since she turned bad girl, she's been a part of The Lifters. Twenty loved her bravery. The last member of the team was a computer geek named Tony, but Twenty called him Tech. They met in computer class. Twenty noticed how good he was with solving problems with engines. Twenty came to him one day and flat out asked him did he want to be a part of the team. Tech being the smartest guy in school without any friends, agreed. From zero friends too three friends is how he looked at it. There were people who cared about him, real friends not computer friends, but real friends at school. Twenty used Tech to fix all the cars they had lifted. If something happened to one of the vehicles while they were on the move. Tech would fix the problem at the garage before the vehicle was delivered to the buyer. Tech was the best and he had the best friends. Twenty went back into the bedroom. He picked his phone up from the nightstand and dialed his best friend's number. Jeff answered in two rings. "Twenty," "Jeff," Twenty took the sheets off a fine exotic redbone. Twenty was addicted to the fast life. Money, cars, clothes, drinking, and his biggest addiction were women. He loved being with a different woman. That's why Paula never hooked up with him except for two times, one being prom night. Paula had turned down every boy at school except for Twenty. He took her that night and they had the best time. Paula knew he was a player and she gave him some anyway. That was her first time. After prom, they decided to go back to their ways. Their friendship was more important. The other time happened two months ago when Paula had her twentieth birthday. They had got drunk and ended up in bed together. Another slip. It felt more like love to Paula, but decided against it. She knew better than that so she bottled it up and kept it to herself. "What's going on man? You ready to get this money?" "You know it," Jeff replied. "Are you?" The girl woke from the chill of not having any covers over her naked body. She looked at Twenty puzzled. Twenty tossed her clothes at her. "Time for you to leave." He pointed to the door coolly. She frantically grabbed her clothes cursing him out the entire time she put them on. She slammed the door with great force as she left that it shook every picture on the wall. "Whoa, crazy." He muttered. Jeff knew exactly what was taking place. He knew about Twenty being the player he was. He was doing the usual, putting another one out after a long night of hot sex. "Redbone from the club last night? "Yeah man, I didn't know she was going to be that damn emotional. I just met her and she knows she doesn't live here." Twenty joked while sitting on the edge of the bed and falling back. Jeff laughed through the phone. "Well, maybe she thought she did. You need to start being more careful." "Why is that?" "These women are crazy. Once they met the guy they really want to be with. He uses her and then she goes five years without dating. Finally, she meets a guy like you all tattooed up, nice teeth and muscles, 6'3, 220lbs, cornrows and great conversation. She figures in her mind, she's met the right guy. Soon as you dump her like trash the next night. All hell breaks loose. Now she's trying to kill you and every corner you turn man. She's there." "Damn," Twenty said. "You described me well. Have we dated?" He joked. Jeff laughed. "You think that shit is funny but I'm telling you man. Watch out. Females are emotional creatures, my man." "Thanks for being my counselor of love. I can handle myself, buddy. I've been doing it for twenty years now. I pretty much got a good grip. Anyway," he got up. He was pissed because he was comfortable. "You talk to Tech?" "He said he'll be at the garage waiting for us." "What about Paula?" Twenty asked. "With this being the last car. I didn't think you wanted me to tell her. The three of us don't need to lift one car, do we?" Twenty thought about that. Hell, he's right. The three of us don't need to lift one car. Really, it would only take the two of them to do it. Jeff would drop him off at the Antique Cars of Atlanta tonight. He would lift a 69' Boss 302 with no problem. The older cars were always the easiest cars to lift. He would race the car back to the garage. Tech would look it over. First thing in the morning Money would be there to pick up the fifteen cars Twenty had stored for him. Pay him the $500,000 owed and it would be simple as that. A piece of cake. Paula could pick her portion up tomorrow when the money arrives. Her job was finished until the next order. "You're right about that. Meet me at the garage so we can go over the final plan and inspect all of the cars again. Tomorrow's the day and we don't need any problems." "Cool, give me an hour and I'll be there." "See ya," Twenty hung up the phone. Out of this deal, he was making $400,000. Everyone else was making $200,000 for the job. That's good money with a team of four. Twenty entered the garage and greeted Tech. He was already inspecting the cars. Jeff came ten minutes later. They spent the rest of the afternoon going over the plan. It started to get late and Antique Cars of Atlanta closed two hours ago. Jeff drove Twenty to the dealer. Twenty saw the beautiful Boss 302 through the glass of the building. "Look at it. That's money right there." "Twenty, man I don't know." Jeff was hesitant. "I got a bad feeling about this one." "Jeff every car we lifted, you had a bad feeling." Twenty got out and shut the door. "Stop worrying. This is the last one and we get paid. We'll chill for a while after this, cool?" "Cool." He gave Twenty some dap. "Be safe, bruh." "No doubt," Twenty vanished into the night.

Chapter 3

THE CHASE

Twenty crept along the building of Antique Cars of Atlanta. He surveyed his surroundings carefully. When he was certain no security was in proximity of him. He made his move further around the building while staying close to the wall. He came to the back door. He retrieved his lock pick tool from his pocket. "Piece of cake." He muttered to himself. The back door wouldn't be any challenge to him. He picked harder doors before. He stuck the lock picking tool in the keyhole and listened carefully as he turned to pick it. He listened for all the correct clicks. He mastered the lock and on the last turn the door popped like magic. "Yeah baby, that's it." He muttered. Before he walked in he did what he normally does before walking through a door without knowing who's on the other side. Maybe security, maybe not. He didn't think security would be lurking around inside of a dark building waiting for him to come but what the hell. Better safe than sorry. He knocked on the door three solid times and ducked off. He patiently waited. Nobody was home. After two minutes he crept back to the door and opened it quietly as possible. He peeked his head in. Look at all these sweet cars just waiting for me to pick one, he thought. He crept in. "Anybody home. I just wanna borrow some sugar or a 69' Boss 302." He joked to himself. He cautiously searched for the area that would have the alarm pad. Tech told him he would have two minutes to disarm it after stepping foot in the building. If he didn't want the police all over his ass, he better get to it. He kept a cool demeanor as he scanned the room. "There we go, baby." He found the alarm pad on the center wall under an oil painting of an old Ford GT500. One minute to go. He hurried over. He flipped the alarm case down, revealing the number pad. "Ok Tech, you fucking better be right or I'm fucked. What were the numbers, 3, 4, 0, 2?" He knew if he got the numbers wrong he would have one more chance. One more chance was something he wanted to avoid altogether. Tech told him if he got the code wrong the first time the pad would beep. Signaling to him he was wrong. The second time it would turn red and the police would be on him before he had the chance to whip his ass. What he needs is for the numbers to light up green, signaling that the alarm was disarmed.

Tech broke into the dealer's computer system and retrieved the code. That's how they were successful at entering dealerships that had cars on the list. Tech is a genius. Without him, it would be a brick through the window and a swift wiring of the vehicle then a fast getaway or prison. He was grateful to have Tech on the team. It gave him more leverage and with the extra needed time. There was no need to wire the vehicles anymore. He'll just find the keys instead. He punched the numbers on the pad. "3, 4, 0, 2." He mumbled pressing each button. The pad made a loud beep. "Fuck." He muttered. One more chance. Get it right or break for it, he thought. "Ok," he raised his hand, thinking about the code Tech told him over and over. "3, 4, 0, 3." He almost broke a sweat. Thinking he was going to have to break for it. The pad turned green after a long second. "Hell yeah." He found the key room without any problem. He found the mini safe with the key to the Boss. He began to pick it. The safe was already unlocked. "Dayum, somebody is going to get fired." He thought it was odd but brushed it off. Time is money. He hurried to the garage to lift it so he could drive the Boss out without any damages. Suddenly, the dealer's lights cut on. He heard freeze! "Fuck!" He rushed to the Boss and hopped in and fired up the engine. Police swarmed the car lot. "Get out of the car!" Daverson yelled. "Twenty!

It's over! Police are everywhere, you're cornered!" Twenty began to realize he was set up. They were waiting for him. What to do? He looked at the glass doors. "I can't go to prison." He floored the Boss and busted through the glass doors. The engine growling through the parking lot. He shifted the motor into high gear. "Fuck!" The police were at the front entrance. He shifted to reverse and burnt out backward, leaving a trail of smoke. He couldn't get far. A helicopter lowered close enough to the ground and blocked the car in. The police had weapons ready for business. He watched his young life go. No choice, he surrendered.

Chapter 4

TRIAL

Twenty knew there was nowhere for him to go. They had finally caught up to him. He rested his head on the headrest in the Boss 302. He exhaled deeply waiting for them to apprehend him. Police cars were everywhere. Two helicopters hovered over the car with their lights directed at the vehicle. He thought about what his best friend Jeff said before he left. He didn't feel right. Out of all of the times he has said that, he was right about this one. The last one for a while, Jeff. Then we can chill, he thought. He smirked to himself thinking about the consequences. He knew exactly who voice it was in the building that told him to freeze. It was detective Daverson. Daverson has been after Twenty for the past three years. Ever since Twenty became a professional car thief. The GTA number went up three hundred just in the area. One hundred and seventy-five of those he believes belonged to Twenty. His signature twenty dollar bill was left on the scene. Pay for what you steal is how Twenty looked at it. He could never catch up to Twenty until now. The tip from the Spokesman put him one step ahead. "Twenty, it's over son." Daverson said. "Hold your hands out of the vehicle and come on with me." He had his Glock aimed at Twenty through the driver side window. Emotions ran through his mind as he still couldn't believe he had been caught. He thought about his best friend Jeff. It was now that he realized he actually loved Paula and wanted to spend the rest of his life with her. He wanted to tell her he's sorry for being a no good dog and for how he treated her. Now, that will never happen. Tech, he wanted to tell him that he really was his friend before he asked him to join the team. He thought he was kind of weird, but cool for a computer geek. The Lifters, his family. "Daverson," Twenty answered casually. "You finally got me, huh? Doesn't it feel good?" "Twenty," Daverson spoke over the commotion. His clothes were blowing from the helicopter wind. "You couldn't run from me forever son. I told you I'll catch you. Now come on and step out of the vehicle quietly and come with me. I got a party to go to." Twenty smirked. "What kind of party is that? Am I invited? I promise I won't steal a car." He joked. "A party for busting the best car thief around. Now, bring your funny ass with me son." Twenty smiled and stuck his hands out of the window slowly. The police moved in on him and removed him from the car cautiously. He saw Channel 2, 5, and 11 news vans out. Reporters were swarming the scene for information on Twenty. They cuffed him on the hood of the Boss 302. Daverson lifted him from the hood. He noticed that all of the police officers were smiling and giving each other high fives. They were excited to bring down the greatest car thief in Atlanta's history. Promotions for everyone. Twenty nonchalantly kept a cool smile watching the SWAT team and the FBI party for his arrest. Daverson shoved him forward. "Chill playa, this shirt is worth more than that promotion you're about to get." Daverson shoved him again. "Told you it was going to be a party. After this, I'm going to bust the rest of your friends. Move your ass son." A reporter approached Twenty with a cameraman. "Is there anything you would like to say to the people?" She held her microphone out for him. Daverson spoke arrogantly. "Yeah, he wants to say he's retired." "We want to know if the man they call Twenty have any comments?" The reporter was struggling with her hair blowing from the helicopter wind. She held the microphone up to Twenty. "Is that any way to speak for a famous person Lenny?" Twenty taunted Daverson. "Yes, there is something I would like to say." He knew by now that everybody in Georgia was watching this or soon will be. There was only one person he wanted to talk to. "I frequently don't do this, but I want to tell Paula I'm sorry. Sorry for everything I ever did. I want to tell you that I love you, Paula. Jeff, you will always be my best friend. Take care of her for me. She deserves a guy like you. Both of you would make a great couple. Tech, you always have been my friend since computer class and you always will, man. Take care, I'm fuckin' out. Holla." They got him booked in and later he made his one phone call to Jeff. He told him the court date. A week later, every one of the Lifters showed up to support Twenty. He faced the judge for the final decision.

Chapter 5

PRISON

Life without the chance of parole. Twenty knew it was coming. He sacrificed his own life to save his friends. They threaten to put every one of them behind bars for fifty years. No one would have a life to live. He cared too much about Paula and the rest of the Lifters. He wouldn't let something evil as that, happen. He manned up and took the one hundred and seven six felonies. One for each vehicle he lifted. He held his head high and sucked his teeth at the judge before turning to his team. They had no idea he just saved them from fifty or more years in prison. He already told Jeff where his savings were hidden. He had a little over 1.2 million from all of the past lifts. Take the money and get out of the game with Paula. That's what he told him. That was his new plan. For Twenty, it was officially over. The rest of his young life would be life behind bars. He noticed Jeff had his arm around Paula soothing her as she grieved on his shoulder. Jeff looked extremely sad while Tech had his head down in his hands. The scene was emotional as he watched the pain over their heads. Jeff turned his attention to him. He smiled at his best friend and nodded. He knew Twenty wanted him to be strong for the team. They would need his care more than ever now that he was gone. The courtroom police escorted Twenty out to the hall. That's where the other inmates waited chained together. Three officers chained Twenty back up and went back into the courtroom. Twenty put his head against the back wall. He heard chatter all around him from the other inmates, but he blanked them out from his mind. All he could think about was his friends and life in prison. "Life." He muttered to himself. The guards came after all the inmates were finished and took them back to the bus. The longest bus ride of his life and it was back to confinement. What a waste of twenty years of living. The sad part was his twenty-first birthday is in two days. His cracked out mom told him he wouldn't make it to twenty-one. Guess the pipe head was right, he thought. She was hooked so bad it was amazing how she is still alive at 46 years old. She kicked him out when he turned 14 years old and haven't seen him since. He knew she was alive for sure. Paula visited her a time or two. He arrived back at the jail. They informed him he was scheduled to leave with the next prison shipment. The judge wanted him shipped immediately. A menace to society is how the judge and the DA label him. Twenty's bus ride to prison arrived one week later. The deputy chained him to a white guy, huge and heavily tattooed. He resembled a biker. Twenty guessed right. The guy he is chained to is a part of a biker gang called, White Shield. They are known for moving ice and prostituting women and young girls. They respected nothing but their kind. The whites. Twenty settled in his seat. He was chained inside, so he took the window seat. He heard the biker snorting. Obviously, he could sense the biker didn't like him. He could care less. He wasn't afraid to hook with nobody. If it came to that, he already had planned out in his mind how he would take the guy. He had a plan for every occasion and every situation. He always did. He sucked his teeth and faced out the window. All he wanted to do was ride in peace to his next destination. He didn't want any problems with nobody. Not even the bus driver. The biker snorted again. He was breathing over Twenty. "You suckin' your teeth at me, nigger?" He was sounding real tough. "I said you suckin' your-" That's as far as he got before Twenty elbowed him without looking. He caught the biker off guard. Blood shot from the biker's mouth all over him. He shattered his front teeth. Pandemonium broke out on the bus as the guards tried to rush to the back. The prisoners were standing in the aisle, making it difficult. The biker groaned. He was feeling light headed. "Ah!" He tried to reach for Twenty. Twenty had immediately followed with another elbow and the biker blacked out. Two swift shots to the face violently. The biker fell forward and his head rested on the front seat. Twenty nonchalantly faced the window until the guards arrived. They were shocked. "What's going on here," One of the guards roared. "He's thinking about prison." Twenty answered the guard coolly while still looking out of the window. The guard looked at Twenty. Twenty stayed facing the window while ignoring him. Minding his own damn business, he thought. The biker was sleep and heavily snoring with his body leaned forward and his head resting on the front seat. Blood was pouring from his nose like a water fountain. The guard hadn't noticed it until a large puddle of blood formed around his feet. Only five minutes into their long trip to Jackson County Prison and the bus had to stop. The guards finally got all of the prisoners to settle back down. Their guns and Tasers came in handy with cruel threats. "Wake him up." One of the guards told another. The guard that was standing in the puddle of blood tried to wake him. He was trying his best, but the huge biker remained asleep, out cold. "Sir," he cried. "He's not waking up."

"Unchain him and move him to the front of the bus. We need to stop the bleeding." He ordered another guard to help him move the biker to the front of the bus. The two guards took ten minutes to move the guy. Dripping much-needed blood from the biker's nose and mouth the entire way. They propped the biker up in the front seat and begun to operate on his wounds while he was still asleep. The bus got back on its course headed to the prison. The head officer spoke to Twenty arrogantly. "If I have any more problems out of you." He was close enough to kiss Twenty on the cheek while he had his index finger pressed against the temple of his head. "Your ass is going to the hole for one month immediately. You'll be pissing and shitting in a bucket and wiping your ass with your hand. I'll make sure of that, believe me." He was sweating ferociously over Twenty. Twenty didn't want to show any signs of weakness to these guards or anybody else at the prison. If he's going to be there for life, they were going to respect him no matter what he has to go through. He moved his head away from the guard's finger and mushed his head away as he spoke. "Man, back your sweaty ass off me. Your breath smells like shit." He said nonchalantly. Then he faced the window. The head officer was furious. He whipped out his Taser and zapped Twenty until he passed out. "Looks like we got ourselves a smart-ass, boys." He laughed and walked back to the front. Twenty stayed sleep the rest of the trip. It seemed like only five minutes. The bus came to a harsh stop waking him up. His vision came back into sight as he looked out of the window. He was looking at his new home. "Fuckin' bullshit." He muttered to himself. He still felt shocks from the Taser. The cage door up front opened and two guards hurried to the back. "You're coming with us." One officer lifted him from the seat. Both of the guards dragged him harshly off the bus. He was faced backward as they dragged him. When he got to where the biker was seated in the front. He violently kicked him in the face busting his nose and mouth back open. The biker was in too much pain to try an attack. He vowed to kill him on the prison yard. The guards threw Twenty off the bus cuffed. He hit the ground and dust covered his face. The guards came off and gave him a good whooping with their batons. Afterward, they immediately dragged him all the way to the hole. He heard one say. "Two months tough guy!" Then slammed the door. "Fuck you!" Twenty yelled. He picked himself up and brushed off. Prison was already hell. This is how he had to spend the rest of his life, in hell. He sat back against the wall and closed his eyes. He thought about what had gone wrong at the Antique Cars of Atlanta. The safe for the Boss 302 key was open. His instincts told him something was wrong then. They were waiting on him. Waiting for him to make a move to catch him red handed. What a setup. He smiled. Nothing to do about it now. Two months in the hole were hell. It was time for him to leave the shit and piss smelling room. The guards came to get him. The fresh air hit his nose and cleared up his breathing. They hauled him out of the hole and dropped him off at his cell after a shower and his medical shots. He entered his cell and the guards removed the cuffs. "Remember boy." One guard growled. "We run this prison." He slammed the door. Twenty sucked his teeth. "Please, we'll see." He muttered. He turned around and a Chinese man was doing pull ups. The Chinese man stopped and stared at him. "John Kim." He held his hand out. "Twenty." He shook his hand.

MY BROTHER'S KEEPER

BOOK I

A Novel

Billie Dureyea Shell

Prologue
JAR SIMMONS

Jar Simmons sat in his office, reviewing some last-minute paperwork. He was in a hurry but had to finish. It's how his family eats. Tonight, he was taking his beautiful wife Noti out on a date for their 20th anniversary. He planned a romantic cruise around town in their limousine. They would go dancing and spend the night together in an exclusive penthouse. Twenty years of marriage and she still holds the key to his heart. He bought her a new 15 carat, emerald cut diamond ring worth one million dollars. The piece was astonishing. He was ready to run out of his shoes to give it to her. Life was good. Jar remembered taking his wife shopping for a new watch on her birthday. It became an afterthought in just five minutes, something else that held her absolute attention. It was a beautiful diamond ring. He stood back, taking in his woman marveling over it. She was captivated. He had to admit the ring was gorgeous. The very next day, he purchased the ring without her knowledge. For two long, hard fought weeks, he kept the ring a secret. She had a way of finding out when he kept something from her. This time, he tried not to look or act any differently. The ring was safe and he wouldn't fall under her spell. A simple touch from her could provoke any man. She was dangerously beautiful. He finally finished the paperwork. His body felt stiff from sitting in one position for so long. He stretched his arms and legs before he got up from the desk, it took him five steps to get to the file cabinet. He put the papers away and then retrieved his coat from the closet by the front door. He grabbed his car keys off the desk and hurried to the exit. Seconds after leaving the place, his feet froze. He stood there, something inside, telling him to stop. He checked the doorknob to see if it was locked. "C'mon." He muttered to himself. He realized he left the ring on the desk. He patted himself down to double check, nothing, then he unlocked the door. After taking a step in, he heard a familiar voice. "It's over," A harsh voice spoke. Jar felt a brutal blow to the back of his head. His legs buckled and he fell to the ground. Somehow, he gathered the strength to roll over onto his back. He couldn't see a thing, everything in view was blurry. He held the back of his head. The feeling of blood leaking through his fingers didn't feel so good. His eyesight regained focus and he was able to see his assailant. "You," He groaned in agony. "I always knew it would be you." The gunman stood firm over Jar and pressed the gun to his face. "I guess you were correct about something for the first time in your despicable life." He smirked. "Please," Jar pleaded for his life. "Don't do this-" He was interrupted. The gunman fired two shots in Jar's face. Large chunks of his head erupted like tiny volcanos filled with blood. The gun exploded a second time. His entire body jerked as if each bullet was a volt of electricity. Three large sections of his suit jacket had disintegrated into the air. His chest settled as his breathing stopped. His only regret was seeing the person who killed him.

Chapter 1
1993

"Jar, wake up!" Noti pushed her husband as her pains grew worse. "Please, I need you." She cried out in agony. The pregnancy was moving into the final stage, labor. This is the worst pain she has ever felt in her life. She calendared the entire nine months. She knew from the day they decided to start a family in March, a baby could arrive in December. Today is a special day, Christmas Eve. And there is not a more painful feeling than labor. She cried louder, wanting to get to the hospital. Jar heard his wife crying while he was asleep. He slowly rolled over to face her. "Hey, honey. What's wrong?" He asked sleepily. She gripped his shoulder and squeezed. "What's wrong," She yelled. "Your child is trying to kill me!" He felt like the Incredible Hulk gripped him by the shoulder. The pain showed all over his face. It was hard to respond. "My... child?" She groaned and applied more pressure to his shoulder. "Yes... our baby is on the way, I need to get to a hospital... now." Jar thought he heard his shoulder pop. He was wide awake, thanks to her tiger grip. She's in labor, he thought. "Shit. You're in labor." He noticed sweat across her forehead. This was serious. He rushed out of bed while she remained lock to his shoulder. He caused her to fall over on her side unexpectedly. His mind started to race. He knew what he had to do. They had taken baby classes together. He remembered the step by step guide he had to master about pregnancy procedures, every meeting he had to attend, and all the training videos he watched. It was time to put his new skills to use. He got dressed quickly, putting on whatever he could find. It didn't matter if the clothes matched or if he had worn them the day before. After he was fully dressed, he found his wife something to wear. He helped her up and swiftly got her ready. He struggled to get her out of the room. When they entered the hallway, he called for his maid, Nina. She came running down the hall to aid them. "It's time?" She asked Jar while giving him a helping hand. She placed her arm around Noti to help support her to the front of their mansion. She was always on standby and alert. She was hired precisely for that reason. During Noti's pregnancy, Jar hired Nina to aid his wife with everything she needed when he was away on business. "Yes, she's in labor. We have to hurry." He responded before opening the front door. They stopped at the front driveway. If he had one wish, he would ask to take away her pain. Every sound she made pierced his heart. He cared about her more than anything in life. "Nina, hold her straight up, I'll get the car." "Yes, sir." She replied. She held Noti firmly in her arms. "Thank you." He said before rushing over to open the garage. He unlocked the Aston Martin, the engine roared to life. He drove the beautiful car back to them and opened the passenger door. He assisted Noti inside the vehicle. He strapped on her seatbelt and closed the door. The hard part was over. He thanked Nina for her assistance before getting back into the sports car. He was on the move and without noticing, slid over the hood of the vehicle like Will Smith in an action movie. He got in the car and sped away from the property. The car raced through traffic as he gunned the V-12 to the hospital. Luckily, the police didn't give him any problems. He pushed the motor well over a hundred. They safely arrived at the hospital. He rushed inside to get help. "My wife is pregnant!" He said frantically. "She's in labor. Please, I need help." Two nurses came rushing out with a wheelchair to assist Noti inside of the building. After what felt like an eternity, Jar witnessed his baby boy being born. They both wanted to keep the gender a surprise until the due date. Suddenly, another boy delivered into the world. They didn't expect twins. Jar never felt a fantastic feeling like this one. He is the father of two wonderful boys. He thought with all the love in his heart to name them. "Let's name them Kane and Abel."

Chapter 2
CHRISTMAS

Jar held both of his newborn boys in his arms, Kane was the firstborn. He weighed eight pounds and two ounces. Abel weighed a solid eight pounds. The boys were identical and looked exactly like their father. Although Kane's hair was a lot longer than Abel's, Kane resembled his father the most because they have similar features. He cradled the boys in his arms, Kane on the right and Abel on the left. He brought Kane closer and kissed him on the forehead, Abel seemed angered by it. He started to pout and began to cry. Every time he kissed Kane before him, Abel would get jealous. He smiled at his son and tried to kiss him. Abel's tiny hand smacked him on the lips. He joked by opening his eyes wide in shock, making Abel giggle. This amused his son and it made him smile. Jar allowed Abel to smack him as many times as he wanted just to keep him happy. There was nothing he loved more than his family. Jar waited with the boys in the recovery room. He stood over the boys while they were asleep. He thought about all the wonderful things in life he wanted to do with them when they were older. He watched two nurses push Noti's bed into the room. He walked over to the door and held it as they guided her inside. They aligned her next to the cradle beside her boys. The nurses told them if they need any assistance, use the controller on the side of the bed, just press the red button in the center. It will send a notification to the nurse's station and somebody will be made available to assist them. Jar thanked them before they left the room. He walked over to his amazing wife of two years. She still looked exhausted from labor. He saw her struggling to get comfortable. He helped by propping some fluffy pillows behind her back. She had worked hard through the pregnancy. He would make sure to be there for her every need, keeping his promise as a husband. A week later, they left the hospital. Jar loved taking care of his family and being there when they needed him. He spoiled the boys. He noticed as Kane grew older, he started to look more like him. Kane's hair grew longer and Noti dreaded it, giving him the same hairstyle. Abel always seemed to get something stuck in his hair. On their third birthday, he managed to find a pair of scissors. He chopped off most of his dreads. Noti found him in the bathroom, scissors in his right, hair in his left. Hair was everywhere, mainly the sink and floor,

Abel had large patches of hair missing. It forced her to shave his head. Since that day, Abel never wanted to grow long hair. There was a time when he tried to cut off Kane's dreads. Noti had stopped him just in time and Abel would use his cute baby voice to get out of trouble. His apologies would cause her to cry. He was the bad one and very close to his mother. She saved him from everything, and he used her to his advantage. Kane was never in trouble. He stayed attached to his father's leg and wanted to go everywhere he went. Noti tried to break him out of it, Kane would cry. When Jar left the house without him, he would cry. Kane would leave Noti if Jar walked into another room. Work was no exception. He brought him on a few occasions. Everyone at the office thought he was a great father for bringing his son. Kane grew on all of them. They treated him like a little brother. On their fifth Christmas, everyone at the office bought Kane a present. When he arrived at home, Abel noticed all his brother's extra gifts. He ran to his mother and cried. Jar explained it was a surprise and didn't know anything about the presents. Later that night, when Kane fell asleep, Abel broke every single gift Kane had... including the extras.

Chapter 3

HIGH SCHOOL -KANE-

It's 2009, my sophomore year of high school. I had grown to be 6'1 and 185lbs. I get along with everyone in the building. They all love me. I'm a beast in three different sports. I play varsity basketball, football and I run track. I love playing ball, but I like running track. That's where I met my first and only girlfriend, Kim. She's a little older but like me. She's a senior and runs for the girls' track team. Man, let me tell you. She's put together. As I got older, I started to take an interest in girls. All my friends have girlfriends. I was the only guy without one. To me, Kim is more beautiful than any girl in the entire school. She has the whole package, a nice ass, breast, gorgeous skin, and a beautiful face. Her brown eyes drive me crazy. And her hair is dreaded like mines. At first, I thought she had mistaken me for somebody else or a senior. I tried to explain to her I wasn't, and she told me it didn't matter. The boys and girls team practiced together. That's when she would bother me. I counted on it every time we stretched before and after practice. She would find a way to get next to me and pull my hair. I used to watch her giggle with her little girlfriends when they spoke to each other. They saw me watching and laughed anyway. I thought something was wrong with me. Later, I learned that it was just a girl thing. My father told me you would know when a girl likes you. She'll do funny shit like pull your hair. That's just the way they act sometimes. When I gained the confidence to ask her out, she answered yes before I could finish the question. That was crazy. It's like she read my mind. My best friend, Simon Jones, is on the track team. He's the fastest person I ever met in my life and we're in the same grade. He ran the forty-yard dash in 4.2 seconds. He won the state title two years straight. I finished behind him with a time of 4.3 seconds. He barely beats me when we compete. The coach said we're the fastest two legs that had ever run for the school. I even gave Simon a nickname and everybody calls him by it, Smoke. When he lines up to run, my boy would say, somebody is about to get smoked. That's exactly what would happen. He'll outrun everybody and I would be the only person who could keep up. Smoke and I took all the titles home. The 100, 200, 400, and the 4x4, we won every race we entered. We even went on a double date for Homecoming. My brother Abel avoided stuff like dancing. A few girls told me he was mean.

Hell, I know that already. What the hell else is new? There is one positive thing about him. He's the smartest person at school. He kept a 4.0 grade point average. He told me only knuckleheads play sports. I asked him if I was a knucklehead? He said yes. I'm in fact, the biggest knucklehead in the entire school. I used to wonder how in the hell did he get all the smarts. True, I have all the skills to play any sport I want, but I'm not nearly as smart as that damn bookworm. My brother and I never get along, not even in school. Our friends belong to two different groups. I hang with the cool crowd and his group made up of tech heads. They all are geniuses. We probably spoke two times out of the entire school year. People don't know we're twins. One day, I came home from practice, and he was locked in his room, crying. I heard him from the hallway. I knocked on the door to figure out what was going on and if I could help. He kept yelling for me to go away. I don't know why, but I didn't. He finally came to the door with a sheet of paper. He held it out to me. It had a grade on it, B plus. I asked, why in the hell are you crying over a B plus? He told me how in the hell he was supposed to take over the world with a fucking B plus. Then he slammed the door in my face. The next day the teacher was brutally beaten with a baseball bat. The alarming part about the situation is that it was my baseball bat. My first trip to jail, murder.

Chapter 4

CLASSROOM LOVE

Two officers walked into the classroom. I was in the fourth period, just another day at school in the middle of taking a test and passing a love note to Kim. Two of my best friends were also in the same class. Bear and Redd. I met Michael Redd while playing basketball for the school. He's the point guard and I play the power forward position. Redd led the state in assists. He can't shoot worth a damn, but he can pass the rock. He's only 5'4 and can dunk a basketball. It's one of the most amazing things I've ever seen in my life. His jumping ability is unreal. I filmed him dunking and uploaded the video on YouTube. During the first week, it gained 800,000 views. That's how he got noticed, good colleges. We've been cool ever since, that's when we became good friends. Now the whole world calls him by his last name, Redd. I met my other friend William Brown on the football field. He led State in our freshman year in total sacks at defensive end, 6'5 and 240lbs. The boy is huge to be in high school, a grown man. Last year, he put a hit on a quarterback that ended the guys› football career. The hit was vicious, paralyzed him from the waist down for the rest of his life. When we're in class and he's mad about something, you can see his muscle bulge like the Hulk. He mainly sleeps in the back of the room, so it›s hard to piss him off. The bad part is he snores loud. One time, he slept for five periods straight, we thought he was hibernating. He looked like an enormous grizzly bear. That's why we started calling him Bear. After being startled, I swiftly pulled my hand away. I didn't want the teacher to think I was cheating because I was passing a note to Kim. One of the officers was black and the other was white, and it didn't look like the mesh together. They walked over to the teacher's desk. She led them back out into the hall. They were taking their time talking about something serious or taking our teacher to jail. I told Kim to stop pulling my hair. I was getting frustrated because I was trying to focus on the police. It was already hard enough to hear with the door closed. Redd is the class clown, so he's brave. When our teacher leaves the room, almost every occasion, he'll pretend to teach the class. When he got up from his seat, I thought he was going to do his thang as usual. Instead, he crept over to the door, listening. Good, I knew he would fill me in on the details later. I tried to get his attention, and he waved his hand at me, signaling to be quiet. Suddenly, I saw his eyes pop out his head like a fish. If there is one thing I'm most certain of is he definitely looked at me when he said, run. He was loud enough to wake Bear out of hibernation. When the officers returned to the room, something told me to move fast and get the hell out of the classroom. The black officer called out my name. "Mr. Simmons." I hopped up, going with my first instinct. They walked over cautiously and tried to corner me. Suddenly, Bear speared the white officer. I know he hates the police, but damn. I didn't think he hated them enough to do that for me. That's my guy. I was on rocket speed, leaving the classroom. I hit the hallway, and my 4.3 turned into a 4.1 on speed boost. I could've beat Smoke. I hit the front lobby, where a dozen other cops waited for me... with guns.

Chapter 5

OFFICER DOWN

The black officer put me in the back of a police car. They repeatedly said a teacher had been murdered, beaten to death with a baseball bat. I pray no one believes I had anything to do with killing a teacher. Me, choosing to go to jail? Hell, no. I'm only sixteen years old. I still need to finish high school and you all want me to go to jail. Hell no, forget about it, I have better things than to be locked away like an animal. The first thing on my mind, call my father when I can get to a phone. He knows a lot of people in high places, and I'm sure one of them can help with this situation. I didn't want to get paranoid and look guilty, so on the ride to the detention center, I just sat back and relaxed. That's where they're taking me because I'm under young. I have to be seventeen to be sent to the county jail. They made all kinds of accusations and kept asking questions I couldn't answer on the ride over. I already knew what was up.

My father told me, white men want to rule the world, and they'll do anything to put a black man behind bars. They feel like we're a threat to takeover. To gain control over us, they have to lock us up and throw away the key. They're not about to throw away my key. We arrived at the detention center. They took me to a room with a table and four chairs. They tried to make me confess to the murder. I wasn't saying a word, the more you talk, the more shit you have to find yourself out of, I won't let that happen to me. They asked, why did I pick a baseball bat as the murder weapon. I don't know where that came from, but I didn't kill anybody. The officers were persistent about getting a confession. They thought I would tell on myself, that's right. I'm young and dumb. I don't know any better, help me. Yeah, I'm smarter than you think. I told them to talk to my lawyer. That's right, sucka. Talk to my lawyer. And by the way... I need my phone call. That's one thing my father taught me. If I ever went to jail, don't let anyone talk you into telling on yourself. Your lawyer should be the first person that comes to mind. Always have representation speak on your behalf. The less you say, the more you have control. I could tell they were getting frustrated. The black officer spoke, "We know it was you. We have your prints all over the weapon. Just make it easy on yourself and tell us what we want to know. We'll cut you a good deal." I saw the look on his face. His expression told me everything he said was bullshit. I knew he was lying. Keyword in that sentence, tell. Tell you what? That I did it so you can throw me under the jail. My father said, watch what goes on around you, and most importantly, people will lie to you, so learn their movements and expressions, and pay close attention to their actions. You'll be able to see the lie before it's told. A good deal would be clear of all charges because I'm innocent. I sat back and listened to them go on and on. The white officer finally gave up. I saw it on his face. He was more than likely tired and getting pissed at me. The black cop gave up a moment later. He said some harsh words to me before he left the room. I heard him say, black people are all the same and when you go to prison, you'll meet the best kind. Whatever, tell that bullshit to somebody who cares. I'm not planning on going to prison. Now that's settled, I need that phone call. I was left in the room by myself for a very long time. They probably thought I would crack after being alone, listening to my thoughts. That wasn't going to push me to the edge, and I don't mind being lonely. I need a clear head. Some other things were on my mind. Like, who in the hell took my baseball bat from my locker? Besides Kim, nobody else knew the combination. She's the only person who knows the code. When we break in between classes, she'll slip in notes and put girl stuff in my locker. Lunch is after the third period and we eat together every day. After lunch, she walks with me to my locker. Then, we'll walk to fourth period. That's our daily routine. I saw my bat the last time I opened the locker. The only other person that comes to mind is... my brother. He also knows the combination.

ABOUT
THE AUTHOR

New York Times & International Best Selling Author Billie Dureyea Shell was born in Compton California and now lives in Ladera Heights with his wife and kids who he loves to spend time with.

He is the Owner of several properties in the Los Angeles area and gives back to his community by providing low income housing to those who need it. He stated "It doesn't matter where you at or where you from it's what you do with your time. There's nothing you can't do if you put your mind to it".